THE FRED FIELD

o   o   o

Also by Barbara Hood Burgess

OREN **B**ELL

*To my true friends
Carl and Dorothy*

• • •

THE
Fred Field

• • •

BARBARA HOOD BURGESS

Barbara Hood Burgess

Delacorte ▦ Press

Published by
Delacorte Press
Bantam Doubleday Dell Publishing Group, Inc.
1540 Broadway
New York, New York 10036

*The poem "Alas for Brave Old Mansions" was composed by
Judge James Campbell on the occasion of the old Cass farm being
turned into Detroit city lots. Source:* Early Days in Detroit, *first
published in 1906, and republished by Gale Research Company,
Detroit, in 1979.*

Library of Congress Cataloging in Publication Data

Burgess, Barbara Hood.
   The Fred Field / Barbara Hood Burgess.
     p. cm.
   Sequel to: *Oren Bell.*
   Summary: The summer after he finishes seventh grade,
Oren is occupied with turning an empty lot into a memorial
ball field honoring his best friend, who was murdered there,
and with finding the killer and making him confess.
   ISBN 0-385-31070-6
   [1. Afro-Americans—Fiction. 2. Detroit (Mich.)—Fiction.
3. Mystery and detective stories.] I. Title.
PZ7.B91648Fr   1994
[Fic]—dc20   93-14260   CIP   AC

Manufactured in the United States of America

June 1994

10 9 8 7 6 5 4 3 2 1

BVG

To Detroit artist Tyree Guyton.
Like Picasso's, his work throws off sparks.

○

To the memory of the late Carl Shelling,
who instructed and inspired scores of young
musicians to give their best to *The 1812 Overture.*

ACKNOWLEDGMENTS

For help and direction from my editor,
Wendy Lamb,
and my trumpet adviser,
Lee Burgess

The boy could have played Gabriel's Horn
if he hadn't had a devil on his back.

Bill Bell
Detroit, Michigan

Prologue

It was high noon in June.

He'd made it through seventh grade still alive, without flunking math. Oren Bell sat on his front steps and surveyed his world. To his left he heard the steady hum of the John Lodge Freeway. Straight ahead he saw the gold-crowned Fisher Building, a queen looking down on her distressed subjects: deserted factories, party stores, and empty houses. The gray General Motors Building and the Wayne State University buildings were soldiers holding the line against want and ignorance. It was a clear day. If he walked around to his backyard, he could see the Detroit skyline and the RenCen on the river. His neighborhood was a grand mixture of different kinds of people and buildings, and Oren Bell was right in the middle of it.

He avoided looking to the right. Since the haunted crack house next door had been torn down, there was nothing but empty space to the end of the block. It was starting to look like a dumping ground. Oren didn't mind living next to weeds and rubble, but the house next door had left some of its evil behind in the space where it had been. He could feel it.

The screen door opened and slammed. His little sister, Brenda, joined him on the steps.

"What are you not looking at, Oren?"

"Nothing. I'm not looking at nothing."

"Are too. You're not looking where the house used to be, because you're thinking about how your best friend, Fred, was murdered there."

"Brenda, give me a break. I'm just waiting for Blue and Whitey to come by. We only got all summer to hang out and we need to get right on it."

Spooky the way Brenda could tell where he wasn't looking and what he was thinking. Latonya could, too, but then she was his twin, and that had to be tolerated. It was true that even on a sunshiny day with no school, he couldn't help feeling spooked about Fred. About how he'd died. Right next door.

Latonya came through the screen door bearing a plate of warm cookies. He took one, but he wasn't going to let it obligate him.

"Oren, when you get through staring into space, there's jobs waiting for you inside."

"Oren's brooding over the house that used to be next door," Brenda tattled.

Latonya sat down next to him and softened. He hated it when she tried to be nice to him.

"I know you and Blue and Whitey miss Fred and blame the house where he was murdered; but, Oren, try to dwell on the good that came out of that house."

"What good ever came out of that place?"

"The good came from my dearly departed ghost Spiro Spill," Brenda said. "He built that grand house, and our own house, many years ago. He was an important man! And his ghost led us to where he hid his golden records, and we'll all be rich when the judges and the courts let us have them."

"Actually, Brenda," Latonya said, "it was me who discovered Spiro's gold records shuffled in with his regular records in the house next door. And then it was Oren who led us to the rest of them hidden in our own attic. Your 'ghost of Spiro Spill' was an imaginary friend who kept you company during hard times this past year. We're grateful that he was there when you needed him, but didn't we agree you don't have a pet ghost anymore?"

"How can you say that?" Brenda screamed. "Spiro lived in our purple bedroom! He built our school, the one that closed. It was named after him! He gave our school a music program that's gone. He left Oren a trumpet to play! The one that's falling apart."

"The key words here are *closed, gone,* and *falling apart,*" Latonya said firmly. "You're nearly nine years old, Miss Brenda, too old to be playing with ghosts."

The red light flashing on top of the Fisher Building reminded Oren of something. "Not everything from the house next door is gone, Latonya."

"Yeah," Brenda said. "The red windows from the top floor are sitting on our dining room buffet. Latonya, I heard you say with your own mouth that those windows were cursed by the devil."

"I might have said that last year when they were part of the evil house. But when Jack Daniels gave them to Mama as an engagement gift, those windows were blessed by their love."

Latonya had an answer for everything, but Oren wasn't satisfied. Brenda went back inside to watch television with Granddaddy, and he took another cookie and kept on staring at the Fisher Building.

"Oren," Latonya continued, "I can see by your sad face that you can't put Fred to rest. I've got an idea. How about another ceremony?"

"You said no more ceremonies." He recalled Latonya's reverse-curse ceremony. She had invented it to save them from the evil house. Each fall before school started, like fools they had to march backward past the house and give a reverse curse with their eyes closed. He hadn't told Latonya that he'd opened an eye the year before. He'd never tell.

"I mean the ceremony where you and Fred and Cousin Dink blew Taps at the cemetery to put Brenda's ghost, Spiro, to rest. That was inspirational and made us all feel better. Think about it. I'm going to let you off from doing the breakfast dishes. You just go with your friends and have a good time. I'm leaving the rest of the cookies here for Blue and Whitey."

"Thanks. A lot." The idea of a ceremony for Fred was interesting. And Blue and Whitey were coming toward him. They both threw their empty Coke cans in the field,

Blue hitting the rock they were aiming for, and Whitey missing.

"Hey, you guys. Don't throw your junk in that field."

"Why?" Blue said. "It's nothing but trash and weeds."

"It's Fred's field," Oren said.

"I knew it. I knew it," Whitey said. "The land where the house stood is still haunted."

"We can do something about that," Oren said. "I got a plan."

Chapter 1

○   ○   ○

One week later.

Oren cleared his throat of the high note that sometimes attacked his newfound deep voice. He closed his eyes for a moment to remember his speech. Latonya had helped with a few of the words, but he had worked out all of the details himself.

"Friends of Fred, we are gathered together to honor the memory of the dearly departed."

"Amen," Blue said.

"Hold the *amens*." Oren went on, "The three of us—Basil Blue Brown, John Wayne Whitefield, and me, Oren Bell—were proud to be known around the neighborhood as 'Fred and the Three Stooges.' This is a private prayer for Fred, our brother who is dead. Fred Lightfoot was smart in math and music and he had leadership qualities. He never had a family, but he had friends who cared about what happened to him. Fred was tempted by an evil house that once stood where we are now standing."

"We're standing in front of where it was," Whitey corrected. "I sure wouldn't stand square on its space. Not before Oren gets it blessed."

"Shut your face, Whitefield. This is dead-serious business," Blue said. "Proceed, Oren."

He continued, "All the kids in the neighborhood were curious about the house, but Fred was bolder than any of us. He went inside the house many times. He was tempted to do business in the house and he yielded to that temptation. The house that killed Fred is gone, but Fred would want us to look to the future. Today, with the help of Mama's boyfriend, Jack Daniels, and whoever else shows up, a ball field will be established on this site. My cousin, Dink, and I will play Taps on our trumpets for Fred; then this field will become the Fred Lightfoot Memorial Ball Field. My sister Brenda is in our house next door making an official sign. Blue's brother and Jack are in there waiting to start leveling and sodding the earth. At this solemn moment we Three Stooges will say a little dedication prayer for Fred before my cousin, Dink, gets here. Dink never liked Fred, and I can't repeat in a prayer what Fred said about Dink on many occasions. Let's move in and join hands. . . . Dear Lord, our friend Fred was a basically dishonest person, but he wasn't bad. The truth is Fred was cool, and we will miss his old Indian spirit. Preserve him in our memory always, and keep us safe from the evil that got him."

"Can we say amen now?" Whitey said.

"Sure."

"Amen," they said, and then sat down together on the

ground and thought about Fred. Oren knew the evil from the house had probably just moved over a couple of streets. Still it wasn't next door to him anymore. It was possible to ignore evil on the next street, but pretty difficult to ignore a crack house when it was prospering on your corner.

"Why don't you just play Taps without Dink?" Blue said.

"We need at least two trumpets," Oren said.

Aunt Grace's pickup truck pulled up in the driveway. Aunt Grace, Dink, and Dink's little sister, Dede, got out of the cab. Dink had his trumpet case, but he followed his mother up the steps.

"Hey, Dork," Whitey yelled. "Over here."

Dink followed his mother inside.

"We haven't got all day," Blue said. "Go in and get Dink the Dork, or start blowing Fred home by yourself. No way I can see where Fred would mind Dink being eliminated from his memorial."

"If Dink didn't want to do it, Fred would have made him do it," Oren pointed out.

"That's true," Blue said. "Go make him do it."

Oren sprinted across the field and up the front steps. He found Aunt Grace, Dink, and his whole family in the living room.

"C'mon, Dink. It's time for us to blow Fred home."

"If you are speaking to my son, Dooley Bell, I don't want him involved in your childish games," Aunt Grace said firmly.

The year before, Aunt Grace had called her son Dink

like everybody else did, but this year she was putting on airs.

"Please, Aunt Grace. C'mon, Dink. You got your trumpet with you." Oren hated how pleading made his voice go high, but wherever Fred was, he deserved more than one horn.

"I never allowed my son to hang out with Fred. Fred Lightfoot was trash. Dooley brought his horn along today because Mr. Shell is giving music lessons in the upstairs flat where I once lived. Mr. Shell will be here soon. Oren, you'd better tell Blue and Whitey to go home. You and Dooley could use some warming up."

"I don't play my horn on haunted fields," Dink said.

Oren looked to his mother for help.

"It won't take long, Grace," Mama said. "I think the idea of a memorial for Fred is lovely. He didn't have a family to give him a proper upbringing, but he was a remarkable young man."

"Lighten up, Grace," Mama's boyfriend, Jack, said. "It won't hurt Dink."

"Mr. Shell likes Oren and Dink to practice together. Couldn't you look at them playing Taps together in the field as practice, Aunt Grace?" Latonya said.

"Let Fink blow his horn in the field, Grace." Oren's granddaddy, Bill Bell, said. Granddaddy had once been a famous trumpeter, so he knew music, but he could never say Dink's name straight.

"I do not encourage weird behavior in my children, like other mothers I could mention."

"What you encourage in your boy is terminal ordinariness," Granddaddy shouted. "Fink Fooley will be performing scales in an upstairs flat when he is sixty years old. He will never get his horn off the pad because he will be the Terminal Ordinary Boy."

"Which will be better than suffering from terminal drunkenness like some near-sixty-year-olds sitting in this room."

Oren thought Aunt Grace had struck too low. Granddaddy had recently been dried out from his alcoholic disease, and he was trying to stay sober one day at a time.

"What does *terminal* mean?" Dede said.

"It means a person is going to die of what ails them," Brenda said. Brenda was the same age as Dede, but she knew more words.

"Dink won't die of being ordinary, and Granddaddy won't ever drink any more Red Rose wine," Latonya said.

"I think it's nice of Oren and his friends to let my brother play in the same field with them. They never did before," Dede said.

"Dooley, you go upstairs and wait for Mr. Shell," Aunt Grace said.

Sorry, Fred, Oren thought. *Even you would have been stopped by Aunt Grace.*

When Dink was gone, Granddaddy said something unbelievable.

"I'll help you blow Fred home, Oren," he said. "Go fetch my silver horn."

The truth was, Oren had never heard Granddaddy

blow anything on his silver horn. He had only heard stories about how Bill Bell had once been a famous trumpeter, stories told to him by Granddaddy himself. Granddaddy hardly had the strength to walk across the room. When the hospital had dried him up from his alcoholic disease, it had dried up most of his spirit. In the days when he had been drinking, Granddaddy always had a lot to say, but now he sat in his easy chair all day stroking Skid, the family cat. Skid was used up from his days as an alley cat and was now content to have someone used up to sit on.

"Get real, Bill," Aunt Grace sniggered. "I don't believe you ever did play that horn, and if you did, the instrument is as rusty as you are."

Oren had seen Granddaddy polish his horn and blow into his mouthpiece, but no music had ever come from it.

"You can do it, Bill," Jack said.

"You haven't been feeling well lately, Dad," Mama said.

"He can do it," Latonya said.

Mr. Shell, their music teacher, walked in and took charge. "Blue and Whitey are waiting outside for the musical tribute to begin. Where's Dink? Let's get with it, men."

"Granddaddy wants to take part," Brenda said.

"That's great, Bill. Hurry. There's a crowd starting to form. You'll be heard all over the neighborhood."

Mr. Shell didn't have any doubts about Granddaddy. Oren breathed easier.

11

"Keep that vicious mongrel hound at bay while I go get my boy. Dooley is not going to miss out on a concert heard all over the neighborhood," Aunt Grace said.

There were quite a few people standing around outside. Mostly mothers with little kids, and some older folks from the neighborhood. Another one of Mr. Shell's music students, Wesley Wrigley Fry, a girl from the 'burbs, had arrived with her parents. The Frys were in clean jeans, the way most white people from the 'burbs dressed. There was a gentleman in a green-striped suit. Pretty fancy. He looked like he might have known Fred and come to pay his last respects. Maybe Brenda would know who he was. She never forgot a face.

The Fred Lightfoot Memorial was turning into a big deal. Meanwhile a small, uneasy feeling kept picking away at Oren. In their family Latonya was the positive thinker, Brenda was the weird but creative genius, and he was the born worrier. Right now he was thinking, *If only once in my lifetime I'd heard Granddaddy play his horn.* He spoke quietly in Granddaddy's ear.

"Don't you think you should warm up, maybe practice a few notes?"

"No, I don't. When a trumpeter has let his lip go soft, the lip can still produce a few pure notes. A practice would ruin my lip for the performance. Have confidence in me, Oren. Taps is kindergarten stuff."

It was true that Oren and Dink could play it blindfolded. All the people stood in a circle around them. Dink bowed like he was going to perform a solo. Last Halloween, when they had played the Taps Trio for

Brenda's ghost, Spiro Spill, Fred, then Dink, then Oren
had played it, then they had all played together. Granddaddy was to take Fred's first part. Bill Bell licked his
lips and brought the silver horn up to his mouth as if he
played it every day. He didn't do any of the real fancy
tonguing that Oren knew he was famous for, but his
notes sounded strong and on target as if it were Fred.
Dink came in next and cracked every other note. Mr.
Shell usually swore at Dink when he did that, but it was
a solemn occasion, and also Aunt Grace was standing
near. Oren came in next and did a creditable job. Then
the three of them played together, and this time Dink
blew it right. The spectators clapped.

Jack had put Brenda's sign on a stout stick. He now
hammered it into the ground. Bold red letters declared
this lot to be the Fred Lightfoot Memorial Ball Field.

"Say a few words, Oren," Mr. Shell said.

What had he left unsaid? "Our friend, Fred Lightfoot,
was fourteen years old when he was murdered. Fourteen years is too young to die." That was all Oren could
think to say.

Chapter 2

○   ○   ○

"It will be a short lesson today," Mr. Shell said. "I know you all want to get downstairs and work on the new Fred Field."

"Not me, Mr. Shell," Dink said. "I just want to work on developing my musical talent."

"You need developing, Dork," Blue said.

"Mr. Shell, what are Blue and Whitey doing in our studio? They're not musicians."

"I invited them."

Oren did want to work on the Fred Field. Once the ground was leveled and sodded and the weeds and bushes were raked away, Jack was going to put up a basketball hoop. It might turn out to be a great summer. On the other hand, he had to guard himself against becoming a positive thinker like Latonya. There were a lot of things that could go wrong.

"Wesley, leave the drums alone. I'm trying to make an announcement." Mr. Shell banged his stick for attention. "As you all know, there will be a big celebration on the riverfront on the Fourth of July."

"The Freedom Festival," Latonya said.

"Right. My summer-program high school symphonic band has been invited to perform on the evening of the Fourth in the bandstand on Belle Isle."

"Wow. Right during the fireworks."

"No, Whitey. Before the fireworks. I've decided to include my Fourth and Hancock Street brass and percussion students in the concert."

"Oh, Mr. Shell, my sousaphone and myself thank you for this opportunity from the bottom of our hearts. We won't let you down," Latonya said.

"I may have to shift you onto a French horn, Latonya."

Oren knew his twin would hate being shifted. Latonya was a solid type, and she would never desert her big rented sousa for a puny horn that was French.

"Wesley, I may shift you to cymbals."

Cymbals might work for Wesley. She was good at clashing and beating things.

"Dink has a reliable trumpet, but Oren, I have a very nice cornet lined up for you."

"I'm a trumpet player and I have a trumpet."

"The cornet is an instrument of the trumpet class, Oren. No big change. Now, we only have a month and we have a difficult challenge. You people are going to take part in performing *The 1812 Overture*. This will mean private instruction three times a week. Practicing every day. When you're ready, you'll practice with the big band."

"Can we hang around and listen if Whitey keeps his mouth shut?" Blue asked.

"Blue and Whitey can be the boom-booms. At the performance we'll have a real live cannon. For practice we'll need a couple of cannon simulators. Next practice will be on Monday at four o'clock. Now, let's get downstairs."

Well, Mr. Shell had sure pulled a fast one. Oren knew that his old Spiro Spill Elementary School trumpet had not been repaired up to the high performance required for *The 1812 Overture*. Missing parts had to be handmade, and that took more money than the Bells had. He knew Mr. Shell had been looking for another instrument for him, but a cornet? Whoever heard of a famous cornetter? After Mr. Shell left, he put it to Latonya.

"Do you care that you're being shifted and shafted off sousa?"

"Sousa will always be my first love," Latonya said. "But, Oren, I am not a one-instrument musician. I don't mind being shifted and shafted around a little bit as long as there's a musical purpose to it. I trust Mr. Shell."

"What about you, Wesley?"

"I don't like being shafted onto cymbals. I guess Mr. Shell has to use his high school drummers first, but I'll be ready if one of them gets sick."

"Mr. Shell didn't shift me," Dink said with satisfaction.

"Me and Blue could get shifted from boom-boom simulators onto real cannons," Whitey said.

Oren considered the fact that Dink had not been shifted. It was a good sign. It might mean that Mr. Shell

shifted only the good students. On the way out to the
Fred Field he stopped at Granddaddy's chair.

Granddaddy had put his silver horn away underneath
the living room sofa, where it lived. He was stroking Skid
and looking thoughtful.

"You did a fine job out there today, Granddaddy."

"I did, didn't I?"

"Are you going to get your lip back?"

"I don't think so. I'm retired."

"Mr. Shell switched me onto a cornet. What do you
know about cornets?"

"Cornets lack the power and brilliance of the trumpet. Smaller bell. Don't have the same range."

It was just what he had feared. Mr. Shell had given
him a cut. The only way to relieve his frustration was to
go outside and pound on Dink, but he couldn't even do
that with Aunt Grace around. Granddaddy looked like
he needed a good rest, so Oren went outside. There was
plenty of work to be done, but there were plenty of
workers to do it. There were actually three city lots to
be cleared. There would be room for a baseball diamond as well as a basketball court. Mr. Shell could fit in
the whole Northwestern Concert Band if he felt inclined.

"Oren," Brenda called. "Come over here and meet Mr.
Marcus Sandman.

Trust Brenda to hang out with any famous people
who showed up. Everybody knew Mr. Sandman. He was
an artist who lived over on Canfield Street and put together artwork out of the fallen houses in the neighborhood. The newspapers said Mr. Sandman's street art

took after traditional African designs, but the man said he was making the neighborhood beautiful for people of all colors to enjoy together. Oren shook his hand and tried to think of something artful to say.

"The good stuff from the murder house is all gone."

"I got most of it, Oren. I'm just making a last check. So far I've come up with a couple of brass doorknobs that were buried under the sweepings. Do you know what happened to those red windows that were on the third floor of the house? Those beauties were a tribute to the art of stained glass."

"My mother bought those. Did you get the house's front door? It had a bad shrunken head for a knocker."

"I got the door and the knocker. That shrunken head makes a real statement. That house was sure something for its time."

Mr. Sandman had smiley eyes that laughed even when his mouth didn't. It was clear that he saw nothing but promise in the beautiful cast-offs from the fallen house. Oren was about to warn him that there might be some danger in recovering its pieces, but he heard Jack calling him.

"It's been a pleasure to meet you, Mr. Sandman."

"Oren, Mr. Sandman says you and me and Latonya can come by and help him work on the Canfield Street Art Project," Brenda said.

"I'd like that. I hope you can find the time," Mr. Sandman said.

Brenda had a way of getting herself invited to places she wanted to go. Oren thanked Mr. Sandman and said he'd be honored to find the time. He joined the weeders. It was nice to see so many people in the neighborhood working together on the Fred Field. The man in the green-striped suit was gone. Aunt Grace had left with Dink and Dede. It was turning out to be what Latonya would call a perfect June day.

Chapter 3

o   o   o

On Saturday morning Latonya said, "Oren, you're in charge of Brenda while I do the cleaning. All you have to do is help her cart her flowers up from the basement and then take them outside and set them down by the front walk. She'll do the rest."

There was always some reason for the whole family to humor Brenda. The winter before, their little sister had been sick. In the early spring when Brenda's pet ghost, Spiro Spill, had left her, Jack Daniels had got this idea that Brenda should have some pet seeds to take Spiro's place. Jack had set up special lights and boxes of dirt in the basement. Brenda had taken right to her new seeds. She had been tending them carefully for months. Now they were blooming up in their little pots. The little flowers were called impatiens.

"Don't touch my buds, Oren."

"Why not?"

"The pods will burst open at your touch. They are also called touch-me-nots."

He touched one just to see. Sure enough. "C'mon,

Brenda. Don't be mad. You got a million of these little critters. This one was waiting to burst out."

"Put Tuffcity back in the house. I don't want him digging around while I'm doing my planting."

He could see that the puppy was going to be a problem. Oren settled down on the front steps to watch Brenda. The street was sure a fine place to be, with their house and then empty lots to the corner. It was almost like living in the country. Better, because there was the city sticking up all around them.

"Oren, I need my topsoil. It's in a big bag in the basement. Don't let Tuffcity out when you fetch it for me."

"Gimme a break, Brenda. I got a life, you know."

He put his life on hold and went back in after the topsoil. Last year it had been Brenda's ghost who had dominated his life. The fact was Spiro Spill, in his own quiet way, had taken over their family, school, and neighborhood. Was it possible that Brenda's impatiens were out to do the same this year? No way. Flowers didn't have the substance of a ghost, but still there were so many of them. Once she was through planting, she was still going to have a million of them left over. How was she going to keep Tuffcity from digging and pulling them up? Oren Bell would be expected to play bad cop to the poor pup's natural bent for digging. He looked into his future. There would be a championship ball game going on at the Fred Field. He'd be next door slapping away at Tuffcity with a rolled-up newspaper.

Mama and Jack drove up in her new van. Him and Jack had helped Mama pick the van out at the used-car lot to celebrate Mama's new job. The van had been driven fifty thousand miles that they knew about. With a little luck Oren would be able to drive it in a couple of years. But who ever had a little luck?

Mama and Jack went into the house, and Latonya came back out with Tuffcity. She sat on the steps beside him.

"Mama and Jack are planning something big, and I know what it is. Brenda, stop your squabbling with Tuffcity. It takes patience to train a pup. Hear me? Patience."

He put Tuffcity back inside and then settled down on his step.

"What's up, Latonya?"

"It's not for me to tell you. Mama will call you in for an official report any minute now. This I can say. Mama signed up for college classes at Wayne State University today. She's going to be a lawyer in eight or nine years."

"I know that."

"Well, you don't know the other."

"What other?"

"Jack and Mama are getting married."

"I know that."

"You don't know the date."

"Sometime this year."

"You don't know the month or the day."

"What month? What day?"

"Children, come in here," Mama called.

Brenda refused to come inside, so they humored her.

Granddaddy and Skid stayed in their lounge chair in the living room.

"Bill, do you want to come in and join us?" Jack said.

"No," Granddaddy said.

Mama, Jack, Latonya, and Oren seated themselves around the dining room table. The windows from the house next door glared at them from the buffet. Sunbeams danced streaks of gold through the rosy glass. When the family sat down for their evening meal beneath the ceiling lamp, the eyes would turn to a mean purple and watch every bite they put into their mouths.

"You tell them, Jack," Mama said.

"No, you tell them, honey."

"We're going to be married sometime next month." Mama looked content. "It will be a small wedding with just the immediate family."

"Oh, please, Mama," Latonya said. "Let's have a real wedding in a church, and you and me coming down the aisle in long dresses. We never had a wedding before."

"Neither Jack nor I have the time or the money, Latonya. Along with my new job I'm starting summer classes. Jack will keep on teaching two days a week at Michigan State in Lansing, and the other five days he'll be starting a new position at the Michigan Humane Society in Detroit."

"Please, Mama. I'll do all the planning and work, and it won't cost much money. You and Jack can just go on about your business. All you have to do is show up. Name a date and I'll get the wedding in the works."

"Why don't you choose the day, Bill?" Jack was always trying to include Granddaddy into family life. Most times Granddaddy didn't care about being included into any kind of life.

"I say we set the date for the Fourth of July," Granddaddy hollered.

"Sounds good to me," Mama said.

"Me too," Jack said.

"We have a concert on the river before the fireworks," Oren said.

"I can coordinate those activities," Latonya said.

"Then so be it," Jack said.

Since he'd quit smoking and drinking Red Rose wine, Bill Bell hadn't had the get-up-and-go to spit. Now, in two days' time, he had played his silver horn and set Mama's wedding date. Oren was amazed.

Latonya had to get on the phone and call Wesley to tell her about the wedding. Blue and Whitey came in the front door and let the pup out. Brenda wasn't shrieking, so Tuffcity must be behaving. Then she let out one terrible scream. Oren rolled up a newspaper and ran outside.

There were kids on the Fred Field, and they had pulled up Brenda's sign. The biggest and ugliest one was holding the sign over his head while Brenda attacked his leg. He was beating on her head with his free hand and trying to detach her mouth from his knee. The rest of the gang were laughing like crazy. Brenda was holding on like some bug who thrived on human flesh.

Oren walked over, Blue and Whitey a step behind

him. "You get back in the house, Brenda. Move. You, too, Tuffcity."

Brenda let go and retreated to her impatiens buds. That was as much obedience as he could expect. Oren put his attention on the invaders. He knew this trash to be the Beubien Street gang from across Woodward Avenue. There were six of them, and they were hard news, but they never messed with Fred and the Three Stooges when Fred was alive, and this was Fred's field.

"This field will soon be open for competitive sports, but there are rules for them who use it." He addressed the big, ugly one with the wet knee, who he knew was called the Goon Eye. It was said that the Goon Eye could stare at you without blinking for an hour. He had out-stared cats and owls.

"We don't play by rules," the Goon Eye said.

"The first rule is, no smoking on the field." Oren kept his voice cool, deep, and steady.

"Yeah? What's the second one?" the Goon Eye drawled, a dirty smile smirking his face. His men smirked along with him.

"The second one is, you don't touch the Fred Light-foot Memorial sign. Not ever."

The Goon Eye wasn't any taller than him, but he was heavier by a ton. He was older, maybe sixteen, and he was a pot head. Probably carried a knife. Out of the corner of his eye Oren saw Latonya come out and make her way to him. He had Blue, Whitey, and Latonya behind him. That was enough to take six pot heads if they didn't have knives.

"We didn't see them rules posted," the Goon Eye said, still not making a move, still not blinking.

Jack and Mama came out on the porch. Jack was a stretch over six foot, but he was more string-skinny than lean. Oren knew Jack would come on strong, but hoped he wouldn't. Jack had grown up in some sissy Methodist orphanage, and he didn't have an ounce of street smarts. The Goon Eye's men moved in closer to their leader, and Oren saw their knives.

An ancient Thunderbird with a dragging muffler came around the corner and pulled into the field. It was Mr. Shell. Better than the United States Marines or the Detroit Police Department, Mr. Shell was the Hulk from Hell when aroused. He was strong enough to teach music to grown high school students. Now he stood firm on the Fred Field beside them. Oren let his held-in breath come out slow, swooshing a wave of calmness through his stomach, down to his toes. The truth was, he had been handling this scene pretty well himself, but he wasn't going to turn down a little assistance.

"You fellows come by to sign up for basketball practice?" Mr. Shell asked like he didn't know what was going on. He was carrying his saxophone case, and it could have held a machine gun for all the Beubien Street gang knew.

"Yeah," the Goon Eye said.

"Officer Brown of the Thirteenth Precinct will be here tomorrow to sign you up. Before you go, men, put that post back in the ground. Our sign maker is going to make a new one for us. This new sign will say NO SMOKING,

NO DRINKING, NO DRUGS, NO WEAPONS, AT NO TIME. This is a ball field and we play ball on it. Understand?"

"Sure, man. Anything you say. Sounds like freakin' fun."

The Goon Eye and his men drifted off. Oren hoped Mr. Shell would let him and Blue and Whitey shoot a few baskets before they got on *The 1812 Overture,* but no.

"We got to get Brenda to the doctor for a rabies shot," Latonya said. Mama and Latonya were forever worrying over Brenda's health.

"A person gets a rabies shot when she is bitten by a mad animal, not the other way around. Right, Jack?" Oren said. Jack was a veterinarian. He ought to know.

Jack looked confused. Oren figured that Jack hadn't had enough reverse cases to make a judgment.

"Oren," Brenda hollered over. "Bring me up some more trays full of buds from the basement."

They all took themselves over to Brenda. Tuffcity was barking and wagging his tail, but he wasn't bothering the buds. Oren began to suspect that there was something funny about those impatiens.

"The Fred Lightfoot Memorial Ball Field is turning into a big responsibility," Blue said.

"You know it," Whitey said. "Mr. Shell isn't going to be around all the time to lend his protection. There's more gangs like the Beubiens around waiting to move in on our territory. Our mamas don't allow us to pack knives. Without Fred we're dead. I think this Fred Field is cursed."

"I'm taking Fred's place as the leader of the Three Stooges, and this land is not cursed," Oren said.

"You're taking Fred's place over my dead body," Latonya said.

"Why don't we go inside and have some coffee and cake?" Mama said.

"I just might bring my Northwestern Band over here for their practices." Mr. Shell rubbed his chin in thought.

"Don't none of you worry about protecting our field," Brenda said. "I'm planting my impatiens all around it, next to the street, all the way down to the corner."

Oren exchanged a secret twin look with Latonya. Brenda was discovering a spirit in her flowers like she had done for Spiro Spill.

"Baseballs and basketballs are going to hit your impatiens, Brenda," Mama said. "And then you're going to carry on about it."

"Once my flowers get to full bloom, they will be strong enough to handle anything that comes along."

The Frys arrived with Wesley, so they all went inside to eat. Mama rang up the doctor, but he seemed more concerned about the Goon Eye than he did about Brenda.

"Mr. Shell, have you been seeing Ms. Pugh?" Nosy Latonya. Ms. Pugh was their former seventh-grade teacher. Mama had warned Latonya to mind her own business, but she couldn't pass up an opportunity to match-make.

"As a matter of fact, Ms. Pugh and I are attending the Fox Theater tonight," Mr. Shell said.

"Would you ask Ms. Pugh if she would consider taking on a tutoring job for the summer? Oren Bell here just narrowly missed flunking math. Mama and I feel he needs serious help."

"Be happy to ask her, Latonya." Mr. Shell looked delighted.

Great. Latonya was out to screw up his entire summer. He would never get a basketball scholarship to a Big Ten university, and it would be Latonya's fault. Brenda excused herself and left the table.

"Where do you think you're going, Miss?" Latonya asked.

"I'm going to mix up fertilizer for my impatiens."

"What's in it?"

"Ground-up dead leaves from the house next door, hair clippings from the last time you cut Granddaddy's hair, some of your homemade soup, and as much spit as I could get out of me and Tuffcity."

"That might work," Latonya allowed.

"Doesn't your grandfather want to eat with us?" Mrs. Fry asked.

"No, he likes to go and nibble in the refrigerator when nobody is looking, or in the middle of the night when we're all trying to sleep," Latonya said.

"Maybe he just don't like eating with them red-window eyes staring at him," Whitey said.

After lunch the music students all trooped upstairs. Dink was sitting in his chair blowing scales to the wall.

Mr. Shell gave Oren his new cornet. It was smaller than his old Spiro Spill trumpet and it had a shiny, cheap look to it. He watched Latonya inspect her French horn. She would find a way to be hopeful about the change. Latonya had her positive attitude. Brenda had her impatiens. Dink had his ordinariness. It was fine for them. Wesley didn't look happy with her new cymbals, and that gave him some satisfaction.

Chapter 4

○   ○   ○

I t was getting late, and Mama and Jack were not home. Brenda was sleeping in the purple bedroom. Granddaddy and Skid muttered and purred to themselves in the lounge chair in the living room. Oren was playing Scrabble with Latonya at the dining room table. He hated Scrabble, but Latonya said the game was to improve his spelling. She had won every game they had ever played. He never allowed himself to improve at games that Latonya always won.

The movie was supposed to be over at ten o'clock. Where were Mama and Jack?

"Granddaddy," Latonya hollered into the living room, "why didn't you come upstairs during music lessons today when Mr. Shell invited you? We want you and your silver horn to be part of our *1812 Overture.*"

"I can't risk it. Carl Shell might shaft me to trombone or worse."

"He might at that," Oren agreed. "Latonya, admit it. You hate the French horn."

"Well, it's no sousa, I'll admit that. Oren, *nincompoopery* is not a word."

" 'Tis too." Granddaddy dumped Skid and dragged

himself into the dining room to defend his favorite word. "Here, look it up in the dictionary."

"Hmmm. You're right. '*Nincompoop:* An idiot, a dolt, a fool.' '*Nincompoopery:* the work of a nincompoop.' Well, Oren Bell, you have finally won a game and you did it with *nincompoopery.*"

"How's your wedding plans coming along?" Granddaddy asked.

"Well, I reserved the church and the reverend has circled the date on his calendar. He wants to give Mama and Jack a little counseling, but they don't think they have the time or need for it. I know I can bring them around on that score. Aunt Grace has offered to take us all to Carl's Chop House for the rehearsal dinner."

"Hold it!" Granddaddy shouted. "Keep Grace out. That woman will screw up the works. Heed my advice, or your wedding will turn out ordinary at best."

Oren was kind of interested in this exchange. Granddaddy had never had the slightest interest in the family's social plans before.

"Our wedding will never be ordinary," Latonya said, "and we don't have enough family to keep some out. Aunt Grace wants to be part of it. Give her a chance to shine, Granddaddy. The reception won't be ordinary. Wesley's daddy is a member of the boat club on Belle Isle and he's offered us the use of his club. What do you two think of that?"

"That's great, Latonya." Oren was impressed.

"The Frys have been using our hospitality, and their girl is always staying over. It's time they paid us back."

Granddaddy approved. "You have a flair for this, Latonya. Get rid of Grace, and the whole thing will come off to our satisfaction. Now, go to the kitchen and get us Bell men our bedtime chocolate drink."

"I'm not here to wait on helpless Bell men without so much as a 'please' for my effort."

"Oren doesn't make the chocolate to my taste, and I'm the senior Bell man in charge. Senior men don't say 'please.' "

There was some logic in what Granddaddy said, so Latonya went to the kitchen. Oren turned to his grandfather.

"Granddaddy, I don't like to alarm Latonya, but Jack has been saying things to me like it would be nice if we would take Daniels for our name after the wedding."

"I picked up on that, Oren. He wants to adopt you and Latonya and Brenda. It's fine with me. It's time that you had a real daddy."

"We had a real daddy, and he was your son. Jefferson Bell."

"Don't remind me. It was with a bad woman that I made that man you call your real daddy. I don't believe the Lord had a hand in it. By the time Jefferson was Brenda's age, he was smashing car windows and grabbing other people's belongings from the passenger seat. Smash and grab, that's all the boy was good for until he was old enough to steal a whole car. After that he got worse."

"It's hard growing up in the city." Oren had heard that excuse given for such behavior.

"He had the same opportunities as the rest of us. He was sent to a fine state school for troubled boys where he was provided with individual counseling and special instruction in performing auto repairs. He won the hand of a decent woman who gave him healthy children he didn't deserve. With all those advantages he still took up with drug pushers for his full-time work. The best he ever did for you and your mother and sisters was to leave you to fend for yourselves in a cold and hungry world. Last story I heard was he was dead, and I am glad to believe it. What reason do you have for wanting to hold on to his name?"

"None, I guess. But Bell's your name, too, Granddaddy. Mama, Latonya, Brenda, and me have always been proud to use it. I bet there are lots of good people around by that name."

"Well, then, be a Bell forever if it pleases you. As for me, I think I'll be a Daniels. Bill Daniels. A Bell by any other name. Give that some thought, Oren."

"One more thing, Granddaddy."

"What?"

"Could you ease up on Aunt Grace?"

"No. Grace and I have a healthy hate for each other."

"Mama says that Aunt Grace was once married to your baby brother."

"That's what she says. I had brothers, but we all scattered early like young crocodiles. If one of them was so foolish as to marry Grace, I can't be held responsible."

"Mama says that Aunt Grace shared with us what she had when we had nothing."

34

"Oren, I hate to fault your mother, but Sarah never forgets a kindness. On the other hand, when unkindness is done to her, she forgets it right away. Latonya is turning out the same. Those two have an attitude that's not safe or consistent with human nature. It is up to us men to keep a little common sense afloat in this family."

Latonya returned with the chocolate. Brenda woke up and joined them. "Latonya, I want marshmallows floating in mine."

"Why aren't you sleeping, Brenda?"

"I can't sleep tight since Spiro Spill left me. Tuffcity is not as warm and cuddly as a ghost."

"Give us a break, Brenda," Oren said. "A ghost is not warm and cuddly."

"How would you know?" Latonya had a point.

Nobody knew as much about ghosts as Brenda did. Sometimes Oren found himself wondering if Spiro Spill had been just a fanciful friend to tide her over till she found a real one she liked better. Living next door to a haunted house must have affected her. When Brenda had been sickly the year before, the doctors explained Spiro away by saying Brenda lived inside herself too much. Latonya questioned the doctor's notion. How could a child's imagination take hold of a family and change their lives for the better? Spiro's treasure was real, wasn't it? He had to agree with Latonya on that score.

Granddaddy and Brenda finished their drink and went to bed. Latonya brought him and her another mug, this time more milky than chocolate. He sipped his and stared into the red-glass windows. He and Latonya looked back like ghostly faces swimming in a bloody pool.

"Latonya, why was it that Mama said she needed those windows?"

"Because they are a beautiful work of art. She's going to hang them on the wall someday when she finds a place for them."

"Well, I don't like living with windows that were once in the house where Fred was murdered."

"The windows were on the third floor, a whole floor away from where Fred's body was discovered."

"He could have been murdered on the third floor and his body taken down to the second floor," Oren said.

"So? Why are you putting an evil spirit to those innocent windows?"

"Brenda puts a spirit to things, and you encourage her in it."

"Brenda knows about spirits. Oren, it's quite an honor for our little sister to work with Mr. Sandman. She's not allowed to go over to Canfield Street by herself. I promised her you'd take her tomorrow."

"Why me? I got my music to practice. Thanks to you, Ms. Pugh has given me percentage problems to work out. Basketball and baseball tryouts are tomorrow at the Fred Field. I have a life, ya know, Latonya."

"Well, then get it organized. Put out the light before you go to bed."

He put the light out. A little moonbeam or a light from a car passing on Fourth Street was all it took to keep the windows watching him. He went to the living room. Granddaddy had gone, but Skid was still there. Latonya said you were not supposed to favor one pet over another, but in his secret inside self, Oren favored the old cat over Tuffcity. He loved the pup, but Tuffcity didn't know anything, while Skid was so seasoned. Jack said that Skid might be fifteen, which was old for a cat. Now that he had no tail and lots of lumps, he needed to be a house cat. Skid didn't mind staying inside where it was safe and the food was good, but he knew what was going on out there in the streets. He was a real attack cat. If an intruder broke into their home, Skid would be their best defense. Oren took his jeans off and lay down on his sofa. Skid came in beside him. Another thing—Tuffcity liked everybody, even Blue and Whitey. Brenda's ghost had belonged only to her. Latonya didn't need anything because she was so smart. Skid kind of liked Oren and Granddaddy best. The cat rested on Granddaddy most of the day, but when Oren finally bedded down for the night, Skid took his comfort from Oren.

The clock in the living room showed the time in the dark. It was midnight, and Mama wasn't home. Jack and Mama didn't usually stay out late on their date nights, because Jack had to drive all the way to Lansing when he left her off. They shouldn't be out late or kissing inside a car. No matter what he said, Jack was not fully aware of the danger. Could he protect Mama?

Latonya claimed Oren had a foreboding mind, which was a stroke more serious than a worrying mind. A foreboding mind ran forward and backward at the same

time and made up horrible pictures in color. Latonya
said minds were like television screens and if you tried,
you could make them turn on good pictures. It was
worth a try.

He thought about the time he and Jack had rescued
Brenda off the roof of their house. He had walked on icy
shingles to save his little sister, while the red eyes of the
house next door had watched and dared him to fall.
What a picture that made. Jack had been right there
behind him, backing him up.

Latonya liked to call up the picture of when they had
found Spiro's treasure in the house next door. She believed that someday the courts would give the treasure
back to them. Latonya pictured them all suited up like
movie stars, going to a college with ivy growing on its
walls.

He squeezed his eyes tight shut and brought up a
treasure picture. He saw a mean old judge sitting on a
high bench, looking down on him and his sisters. This
picture was in black and white. The judge wore a black
robe. His white skin was the color of dead fish. He had
black, beady eyes and a long gray beard. "You Bells forget the treasure. Hard labor and sweat will put the likes
of you through college."

He heard Jack's car drive up. Why didn't Mama and
Jack take the van? Driving a Mustang on Fourth Street
was like saying to the Goon Eye and his men, "Smash
my window and rob me. I'm some poor fool from the
'burbs." The key turned in the lock. The door closed
quietly. He could smell the light flower scent of his

mother passing by his sofa. He heard Jack's Mustang fire up and leave. They had all lived through another day and they were together.

Dear Lord,
Thank you for carrying Mama and Jack
back home.
I knew you could do it.
Your friend
Oren Bell.

Chapter 5

○   ○   ○

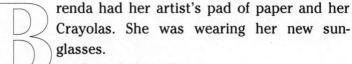renda had her artist's pad of paper and her Crayolas. She was wearing her new sun-glasses.

"Oren, let's go."

"Listen, Brenda. We don't stay more than an hour."

"We do too. Aunt Grace says she'll stop by at three o'clock and give us a ride home."

"Are we invited for lunch, or what?"

"Latonya packed a lunch for us. She says for you to mind your manners."

"Maaaaaan. It might as well be winter all year long for what good summer vacation does me. Why is Aunt Grace picking us up when we could easier walk home? Answer me that, Brenda?"

Brenda didn't pay him any attention. She bobbed along ahead of him down the street. At West Forest they came upon the Goon Eye. This was not the Beubien gang's turf. Woodward Avenue was the dividing line. This was the second time the kid had challenged him on his own side of Woodward. The Goon Eye was sitting on the curb by himself with a rock in his fist. Maybe he was waiting for a bus, since the Goon Eye was famous for stoning buses.

"Hey, Oren Bell. Wait up."

Oren stopped. If they didn't, he would follow them. Besides, the Goon Eye didn't start getting dangerous until later in the day, and never when he was without his men. It was strange that he was up and out this time of the morning.

"Look here, Oren Bell. My men want to shoot some baskets on the Fred Field this afternoon. You don't have to worry none. I'll keep them in line."

"I'm not worried. The Northwestern High School Band will take their practice next to the Fred Field. The average height of a Northwestern band member is seven feet seven. They are under the command of Mr. Shell, our main Music Man."

"You all going to shoot baskets to music?"

"You don't like it, you know what you can do."

"I like it, man. We'll come by and play by the rules. What you and the little girl doing out so early?"

"We're invited to contribute to the Canfield Street Art Project under the command of Mr. Marcus Sandman," Brenda said grandly. "Mr. Sandman is our main Art Man."

The Goon Eye looked to be impressed. He didn't heave the rock at them, but let them pass.

It was an easy, warm day along Fourth Street. They passed a lady dressed for the night. Oren knew she was headed for Cass Avenue, but that was her business. When he thought on it, Latonya and Mama must trust him a lot to let him take Brenda on such an outing. It would sound crazy for him to say to the people they met along the way, "Good morning. I'm Oren Bell, the protector of my little sister," so he said it to himself.

Mr. Sandman had expanded the Canfield Project from when Oren and Brenda had seen it. There were more boarded-up houses on his block for him to work on. Oren and Brenda walked down the middle of the street staring at the wonder of it all. It must surely be better than Disneyland. There were toy trucks and bicycles growing out of trees, and old shoes and roller skates walking up the side of houses. Discarded dolls stared out the windows of an empty house like lost children. There were brightly painted oil drums with tires for hats, marching together in a line like tin soldiers. There was a huge sculpture of an African boy riding an elephant made out of throwaway tin cans. There was a small Christmas-decorated pine tree growing out of a kitchen sink. Wherever a person looked, there was a recycled object to delight the eye and tickle the soul. They found Mr. Sandman in his outdoor studio. He was too involved in his work to notice them, so they walked over and took a look at his canvas. The front door from the evil house was propped up on a tree next to him. It wasn't as though a door was as all-seeing as the red windows from the house, but still Oren had the feeling that the door was watching the artist work. At least the shrunken-head knocker was showing an interest.

"Mr. Sandman," Brenda said. "That's a portrait of the house that used to sit next to us."

"I'm pleased that you recognized it, Brenda. I'm painting my impression from memory."

It was the house, all right, but it wasn't created right
on. When you kept your attention on the canvas, you
saw more than you did at first. The dark building in the
picture was awash on a sea of misty colors like it was
coming at you out of a dream, and the bloody eyes on
the top floor were glowing like beacons in the night.

"Why are you painting that house, Mr. Sandman?" he
said.

"It had interesting architectural shape and features,
Oren, Gothic Revival from the late Victorian period. I
emphasize the height to point up the arches, the chim-
neys, and the beautiful stained-glass windows. My impression, if you see it, could be a ghostly image of past
glory. Or not."

"My late ghost, Spiro Spill, built that house, and he
would be pleased that you're giving it a ghostly impression," Brenda said.

Oren didn't think it was a good idea for Brenda to
share the story of her late ghost. It was common knowledge that the house had been a crack house, but not
everybody knew about Spiro Spill.

"I am preserving the dream for Spiro," Mr. Sandman
said.

He wiped his hands on a paint-spattered rag and
turned his attention full on them. "Ah, yes, Oren and
Brenda, my art students for the day. Better to get right
to the work at hand. There's a bus load of people from

outside the city coming by to watch our project in process. I hope they won't throw off your creativity."

"Not mine," Brenda promised.

Oren hated to deceive Mr. Sandman. "Brenda is the artist, but I don't have any talent in that direction, sir."

"You have the eye and hands of an artist, Oren," Mr. Sandman said.

"He doesn't draw as good as me," Brenda said. "But I'll help him out."

Mr. Sandman's wife came out and introduced herself. When Granddaddy met a pretty lady, he classified her by shape and skin shade. He would say that Susan Sandman was coffee color with a dash of milk and honey, and her shape was just right. Oren recognized her immediately as a fellow worrier. She had a warm smile that said, *If you are a friend of Marcus's and of the art project, you are welcome, but if you are not—tread lightly.* Susan gave them aprons to protect their clothes. A sack that had once packed a hundred pounds of potatoes was Oren's apron. Brenda wore a man's cast-off shirt. Mr. Sandman didn't throw anything away.

He took them down the street to a house that had been empty and down on its luck for a long time. The front porch drooped like a sagging chin. Its windows were all boarded up, so the house no longer had to look at what was going on in Canfield Street.

"There's a lot of cleanup work to be done, but I can't expect artists like yourself to do that," Mr. Sandman said.

"We'll do it," Oren said.

"I'll plant impatiens up and down the walk. Can we paint our house with our own impressions?" Brenda asked.

"Free license. Clean up and create at your pace and judgment. The city has quite forgotten this poor old girl." He waved and went back to his painting.

It was amazing. Their own deserted house to make into an art project. Latonya was going to want a piece of this deal. She might be useful in the cleanup part, but she didn't have the eye and hands of a true artist like him and Brenda. Latonya would want to make the house warm and cozy, so a family could move inside, but it was up to him and Brenda to turn the house into an art object for the city and world to enjoy forever.

After an hour of raking and sweeping, Oren said. "Let's see if we can get started on the more creative stuff. This old wood could use some paint to keep it from rotting."

"Painters need to paint," Brenda agreed.

They sought out Mr. Sandman.

"A paint warehouse donated some interesting discontinued colors," he said. "Artists deserve high-quality materials."

Oren climbed up the ladder and picked up his brush. The paint cans said "Sunburst Orange" and "After Midnight." Why would any warehouse discontinue orange and black?

"You know what I want to do, Oren?"

"No, what?"

"There's a box of old picture frames over out back. I want you to nail them to my part of the house; then I'll paint pictures inside."

"I'm up on a ladder now, Brenda. Just keep working on your black stripe, and we'll do the picture frames later."

"I'll nail them for her," Blue said.

He looked down and saw Blue and Whitey.

"Can we help, Oren?"

"Sure, but you have to take direction from me and Brenda because we are the primary artists on this project. Blue, you go around to the other side and nail up frames where Brenda tells you. Whitey, you take over and finish her stripe."

"I like orange and black stripes on a house," Whitey said.

"It does make a statement, doesn't it?" Oren agreed.

At noon they sat on the grass and unpacked their sandwiches. Latonya always made enough for whoever showed up to share. Susan Sandman brought out a pitcher of iced lemonade. Oren enjoyed his lunch and the view of the project. There were three buildings on the street that were still being lived in.

"Who lives in those houses?"

"Crack houses, for sure," Whitey said.

"Maybe, maybe not," Brenda said, "but not that one on the end. It belongs to a church friend of Aunt Grace. That's why Aunt Grace agreed to pick us up."

A man came out of one of the houses, got into a car, and drove off.

"Who is that?" Oren said. "He was at Fred's memorial and he looked familiar. He was wearing that same green-striped suit."

"He's one of Fred's foster daddies," Brenda said.

"How can you remember that?" Blue said. "Fred went through more foster parents than anybody could keep count."

"I'm a number genius and I never forget a face," Brenda reminded them.

After lunch Latonya and Wesley walked over to see what was going on. Wesley's father was supposed to bring her over for band practice, but the girl was showing up earlier every day. There was never much going on in Grosse Pointe, where Wesley lived. Oren assigned Wesley to go work on Brenda and Blue's side of the house. Latonya wanted to stay with him and Whitey. Right away Latonya started messing with his head.

"Oren, I don't believe the stripes should go sideways. I have to lie on the ground on my side to see what statement they make. They should be going up and down."

"Up-and-down stripes are too hard to do."

"True art takes a little longer, but the satisfaction we will receive from it will make the effort worthwhile."

"Why don't you just go along and tidy up the inside of the house?"

"Why don't you just hurry over and get another ladder from Mr. Sandman so we can make those stripes stand up straight and proudly face the world?"

After a while he left Whitey and Latonya to their up-and-down stripes while he inspected the house. He thought Mr. Sandman would be pleased. Brenda was working by herself in the front. She had a big frame nailed up by the front door, and she was painting in a black *Welcome*. Blue and Wesley were doing the whole side of the house in solid black. Another day when the paint was dry they planned on putting an exploding orange sun in dead center. He went back around and started painting stripes. Thanks to Latonya, their side of the house was going to have the appearance of a jail room. He hated to admit it, but Latonya was right. A jail theme was a good idea. Maybe Latonya would let him make little orange things looking out from the bars.

They'd been working a couple of hours or more when a whole bus load of people showed up. People of all ages stood around and watched them paint. The leader of the bus hollered to the crowd, "Observe the inner-city artists here at work on the Canfield Street Project."

Another bus pulled up filled with kids. Oren and Latonya's seventh-grade teacher, Ms. Pat Pugh, was in charge. She had a summer job at the Art Institute taking children on cultural outings. It was good to see Ms. Pugh in action again. She herded her own boys and girls into orderly lines, and then she went to work on the bus load of adults. Their leader let her take over. It was a wonder how a small lady knew how to make people of all sizes, ages, and colors behave and listen. When she had the attention of the crowd, she started her talk.

"Many houses on this street have been neglected, but observe how Mr. Sandman's protégés are carefully bringing discarded items together to become symbols of the past glory of the street and the neighborhood. The orange-and-black house on your right is particularly interesting."

"Isn't painting pictures on the outside of houses a form of African folk art?" one woman said.

"Yes, ma'am. Mr. Sandman is combining cast-offs from our present-day life and making jewels out of junk." The crowd followed her down to the next house. Some stayed to watch the artists.

Oren didn't let fame interfere with his work. He kept a steady stroke on his stripe. Someone said, "I believe the black stripes are pathways from the past to the future. How clever."

Ms. Pugh started teaching anybody who got in her path, but the stuff she told you had a strange way of sticking in your head and connecting to other ideas. He remembered when she had taken the seventh-grade class to the place on the river where old Governor Lewis Cass's house had once stood. They had memorized a little poem that a Detroit judge had said more than a hundred and fifty years ago on the occasion when Governor Cass's house had been torn down and his farm turned into city lots.

Alas for brave old mansions
Alas for ancient fame
Old things make room for the present
And ashes follow the flame.

Aunt Grace, Dink, and Dede showed up on time like they always did when you didn't want them to. Aunt Grace's friend came out of her house to make comment.

"Do you see what is going on here on Canfield Street, Grace?"

"I do, Dora Dillworthy. Outsiders coming by to gawk at junk. The whole block is covered with junk. I am offended by it. When I am offended, I take action. I'm writing a letter to the mayor."

Without a polite word to Mr. Sandman, Aunt Grace hustled them into the back of her truck. They waved to him as they drove off. "We'll be back tomorrow," Oren yelled.

"Your mother had better not write no letters to the mayor, Dink Bell," Blue said. "She knows zippo about art. Why does she have to take an interest? She doesn't even live on Canfield Street."

"Nothing stops my mother from writing letters to the mayor," Dink said.

Mr. Sandman had given Brenda a piece of canvas and some little tubes of paint to take home. She hugged her new art supplies to her chest and looked mean and worried.

"My father says Mr. Sandman is an important artist and our city is lucky to have him," Wesley said. "Maybe we should start writing to the mayor to cancel out what Aunt Grace does."

"You're all forgetting an important fact," Latonya said. "Aunt Grace has been writing letters to the mayor for years, and His Honor has never responded to a single one of them."

"The mayor probably thinks she's some kind of psycho," Whitey said.

Oren knew Aunt Grace was no psycho, but she was loud and tireless. Granddaddy always said it was persistent loudmouths who got to run any show.

"Since Mr. Sandman is an important artist, the Canfield Project is safe from Aunt Grace," Latonya said.

There was Latonya's positive attitude working overtime again. The year before, she had claimed that Mama's employer, the J. L. Hudson Company in downtown Detroit, was safe forever. Now the J. L. Hudson Company was an empty ghost building covering two city blocks.

The truck came to a stop in front of the Fred Field, and they all piled out. Blue and Whitey had lost interest in being boom-booms for *The 1812 Overture,* so they decided to practice their hoop shooting.

"Oren," Brenda said, "tomorrow we have to take some impatiens over to Canfield Street. They can surround and protect our project."

"Sure." How was he going to carry a load of plants? He supposed he'd find a way.

The musicians went up to the studio to practice. As he took the cornet out of its case, he thought, *What if the mayor does start to read Aunt Grace's letters?* He didn't believe flowers had power, but if Latonya, Blue, Whitey, and Wesley all pitched in, they could help Brenda get her flowers over and planted tomorrow.

Chapter 6

○   ○   ○

The next day Latonya and Wesley were too busy with wedding plans to help plant flowers. Blue and Whitey liked to sleep late on vacation days.

Brenda carried the fertilizer, which didn't smell too good. The streets were deserted, but when they got to Forest Street, there was the Goon Eye sitting on the curb. Oren's guess was that he hadn't gone to bed yet. His big round eyes focused on them with some effort, and then he gave them a sick smile. He didn't have a rock in his hand. The Goon Eye was looking mellow. Likely he had enjoyed some pot with his morning corn-flakes.

The afternoon before, the Beubien Bad Boys had shot baskets on the Fred Field, and the Goon Eye had kept his men in line. Latonya gave her brother credit for restoring a kid to society who had been a dangerous bum for all sixteen years of his good-for-nothing life. Oren knew that one afternoon was not a total reform, but it was a start.

"What you and the little girl doing?"

"We're taking flowers to the Canfield Street Project," Oren said.

"They're impatiens," Brenda added.

"You not movin' them little flowers as fast as they like?"

"Impatiens is their name," Oren said.

"Your little sister the one who talks to ghosts?" The Goon Eye was following them down the street like a big, interested bear.

"When one is around, she talks to it," Oren admitted.

"What about these little flowers who got no patience? She talk to them?"

"Sure I do," Brenda said.

"Can I help you move them flowers?" The Goon Eye was downright pleading. It was kind of pitiful.

"Sure," Brenda said. "You can help us, Skyler."

"His name is Skyler?"

"Skyler Sims," Brenda said.

Oren stopped. How did Brenda know the Goon Eye's proper name? Nobody else did. Oren transferred half of his load of baby flowers to the eager hands of Brenda's new admirer. Skyler held them like they were human buds who might cry if he handled them the wrong way.

The Sandmans were getting ready to take off for an art show in Ann Arbor. Mr. Sandman left Oren as responsible adult in charge. He was given the keys to the paint shed. Mr. Sandman must have heard of the Goon Eye's reputation, but still the man trusted Oren. Mrs. Sandman gave him a police number to call if any vandals threatened the project.

"I think we'd best get the flowers planted first, Skyler," Oren said. "Then we'll show you how to be an artist."

"I don't mind the little girl calling me Skyler, but I'm the Goon Eye to you, Oren Bell."

"I don't have a problem with that."

It was nice to have his hands in dirt. The sun warmed the back of his neck. The Goon Eye had a bent for planting. He knelt on his great round knees and gently put the roots in little holes. Brenda must have had confidence in them, because she was off by herself painting inside her picture frames. Who would have thought he would be kneeling next to the Goon Eye planting a garden?

"I knew Fred, too, ya know," the Goon Eye said.

"Everybody knew Fred." It bothered him a little to share Fred's memory with a kid who had always been trash, by the standards of decent people.

"Fred was more like me than you," the Goon Eye said.

"How am I?"

"You got mother and sisters. You're straight. You'll be still going to school when I'm used up and dead. Dead like Fred."

There was some logic in what he said. Fred had been mixed up in the same kind of activities as the Goon Eye. They had both been foster kids with no family to own them. The resemblance stopped there. Fred had been smart. Fred had been handsome. Fred had had musical potential and he could do figures in his head. Fred had been able to read books with no sweat. Fred had picked Oren Bell for a best friend. Given more time, Latonya,

Ms. Pugh, Mr. Shell, and all of Fred's friends could have helped him to be somebody. The Goon Eye never had much going on between his ears, and he was ugly. His only friends were dropouts and dope heads.

"You planting them little flowers too close one to the other, Oren. You got to give them room to spread out, then they'll cover ground like the little girl wants. You Bells are all one funny family, planting flowers around boarded-up houses. Fred used to tell me how he watched you all from the top floor of the evil house next door to your house. The one that got knocked down."

"Fred told you that? Fred watched us?"

"He used to watch you Bells out of them red windows; you all planting flowers, raking around, getting fussed over by Latonya. He said it was like looking at family life through rosy-colored glass."

Oren shivered. He remembered all the times he had looked up at the red windows and imagined that the house was watching them, but it hadn't been the house watching them, it had been Fred. The oneness of Fred and the house was getting mixed up in his head. He nestled a bud in the cup of his hand and gazed at it. The summer before, he had spent near to every day with Fred. So had Blue and Whitey. Sometimes they met Fred at a secret time and place, because their families got nervous when they spent too much time with him. Fred always acted like he was glad he didn't have a family to lay rules on him, and his Three Stooges envied his freedom. Fred was good times, but he taught Oren, Blue, and Whitey how to stay alive in real life. Ways their mamas didn't know about. Dear God, Oren prayed to the flower in his hand, I miss Fred.

"You're going to squash that flower," the Goon Eye said.

"I'm going to find Fred's killer and put him in jail forever."

"Forever?" The Goon Eye shook his head.

They finished the planting in silence.

When it was time to give the Goon Eye some lessons in art, Oren told him to put a second coat on the black stripes.

"Why we puttin' prison bars on the side of this old house?"

"They could be paths. Latonya says if people who see our stripes believe that they are bars, the other three sides of the house will offer them freedom. Of course people have to have the sense to walk around and look."

Oren went about nailing up the rest of the picture frames for Brenda. Before noon they were cleaning up to go home. He noticed Mrs. Dora Dillworthy coming out of the same front door as the man in the green suit.

"You know those people, Goon Eye?"

"That's old Dora Dillworthy and her man Tedfield Jones. Dora and Teddy were onetime foster folks to me, and to Fred, too, at a different time. That's why I know this neighborhood."

"Do they live in two separate houses?"

"Sometimes Dora kicks Teddy out, and he goes into the empty city house next door. Dora is a righteous woman, and Teddy is a sometimes useful, sometimes useless man."

"Why does she keep him around?"

"Best she can do, I guess."

Oren sensed that there was something else that he wanted to say, but thought better of it. The Goon Eye's big round eyes took on the fixed expression of a Halloween pumpkin that didn't know anything and wouldn't tell if it did.

"Come around by the Fred Field later and shoot some hoops," Oren offered.

The Goon Eye turned and moved off down the street without a word or a wave of his hand.

Latonya was practicing when Oren and Brenda got home.

"Oren, you were right about this French horn. It's not as friendly as sousa. I've about wore out my mouth, and my notes are still going splaaat. Mr. Shell is bringing his band over this afternoon to practice with us, and you know how perfect they all are. They've been to music festivals and marched and played in Thanksgiving Day parades. You're doing better by your cornet than I'm doing on my French horn. I'll be the one to disgrace the family."

"It's the mouthpiece that's giving you trouble, Latonya." Granddaddy said. "The mouthpiece of the trumpet and cornet are close in size. Going from sousa to French horn is a bigger step for you than for him. Let Oren help you."

"Oren, come blow into my mouthpiece. I'd be grateful for advice."

He didn't like trading spit with Latonya, but the opportunity to give her some advice was too good to pass up.

A loud noise invaded the neighborhood like some kind of spaceship had landed in the Fred Field. Oren and Latonya ran outside. A Detroit Public Schools bus had pulled up. The Northwestern High School Band jumped from the bus, its members blowing their horns, beating on their drums, and giving the Northwestern school yell, which was terrible to hear. Mr. Shell was somewhere in their midst shouting orders. There was a lot of swearing going on, some coming from the band members and some from Mr. Shell.

"Don't worry, Latonya. If you crack a few notes, Mr. Shell won't swear at you. He never swears at girls or ladies."

"Mr. Shell is a fine man for you to model yourself after in action, but not in words. You get my meaning, Oren?"

The band was finally settled next to the Fred Field. Wesley and her father arrived carrying her big bass drum. There were maybe ten kids shooting hoops on the Fred Field. Three of them were Blue and Whitey and a straight-enough kid from the neighborhood. The rest of the players were Beubiens under the command of the Goon Eye. This meant that there were Beubiens playing on the same side as the good guys. There weren't enough good guys in the neighborhood to make up a team. Everybody seemed to be getting along, but how long was that going to last?

Mr. Shell shuffled them in with his high-flying band. They had the music, but they were not expected to play it. He told them to stand there and go along with the notes in their heads. That seemed easy enough. There were four other cornets, and Oren was the end one. Dink was on the end of the trumpets. Oren turned around and picked out Wesley standing next to the real bass drum player. She waved to him. Latonya was the only French horn player on the field, so Mr. Shell told her to go ahead and play for real. Mr. Shell was always putting too much pressure on the poor girl. Oren knew if his twin had old sousa, she would do it right. Mr. Shell raised his baton. The Northwestern High School Band took off like they were going to a fire. Mr. Shell's arms just couldn't keep up with the music. He kept bringing his arms down to stop them, but they were going too fast to stop. Finally the band started to shut off, one section at a time, down to the last horn, until the only sound left on the field was Latonya. Splaaaat. Splaaaat. Splaaaaaat. Oren gave Mr. Shell a lot of credit. The Music Man didn't swear. He just smiled a sad little smile and told them to take it again from the top and slow it down. The next ten times they went too slow. By the time they got to a speed that Mr. Shell approved, Oren thought he knew how to play it. Him thinking that was coincidence because Mr. Shell told the Fourth and Hancock Street musicians that it was time for them to come in. Oren gave a nod of satisfaction, and Wesley gave a cheer. Latonya looked determined, and Dink looked ordinary. Mr. Shell raised his baton and started the music. The sounds of *The 1812 Overture* resounded over the Fred Field and beyond. Mr. Shell stopped them when they had done as much as they knew how. The hoop shooters clapped and hoo-hooed.

"We still have a lot of work to do, people," Mr. Shell said. "But you're starting to sound a little better."

Brenda ran out and handed Mr. Shell her freshly painted sign for the Fred Lightfoot Band Field. The Music Man pounded the sign into the ground, and everybody gave another cheer.

It was late, but him and Granddaddy and Jack sat around the dining room table wondering when they were going to get their snack and mug of chocolate. Latonya was still cleaning oil off Brenda's fingers. When Brenda had worked in Crayola, it had been neater. Last year Brenda had specialized in drawing sad sinking or sunken ships. Now she was painting ghostly buildings. Mama was in the kitchen doing homework for her class at Wayne State University.

"I'll heat up the chocolate and throw some cookies on a plate," Granddaddy finally volunteered.

Oren watched him go. There was always the fear that Granddaddy had a little something hidden in the kitchen to juice up his chocolate. So far Granddaddy had stayed sober one day at a time, but it wasn't wise to put the burden of too much trust on a man who had been boozing since he was Brenda's age. Still, Mama was in the kitchen.

"I need to talk to you," Jack said.

Was Jack going to get on him about that name-changing business again?

"Oren, you know this house has been condemned by the city to be torn down."

"It's been condemned for years, Jack."

"There's a city order to take it down by the end of summer."

"Don't worry. There's been city orders before. Besides, Brenda has the place surrounded with impatiens."

"Well, someday soon this old house will come down."

"Get real, Jack."

"Next month at this time we'll all be a family, and I'll be the father. I'll be working in the city, but I need to return two days a week to my teaching job in Lansing. I'd like to see you, your mother, and your sisters living in a safe situation when I have to be away overnight."

"We know how to take care of ourselves where we are, Jack."

"Sarah and I want you and the girls to go apartment hunting with us sometime soon. Will you talk it over with them, Oren? I have a long drive ahead. I don't think I'll stay for the chocolate and cookies."

"You go ahead, Jack."

Jack went out to the kitchen to give Mama a good-night kiss. Jack was afraid to confront Brenda and Latonya with his twisted ideas on where the family

should live. Latonya said apartments were the bottom
of the pit for living. Poor Jack had good-paying jobs and
he didn't beat up on women and kids, but the guy had
no sense. Never had any. Never would. Did he think that
Latonya would give up their home? Did he think that
Brenda would let her impatiens go when they were in
full blossom? Did he think that Oren Bell would ever
give up the Fred Lightfoot Memorial Ball and Band
Field?

Granddaddy screwed up boiling the milk, so he just
shuffled off to his room, muttering at the way the
women in the family were not doing right by him. Mama
closed her books and went to bed. Finally Latonya had
Brenda cleaned and settled for the night. Then Latonya
set a mug of chocolate in front of Oren and sat down to
sip hers.

"Why are you staring into those windows, Oren?"

"Because you propped them right up in front of
where I always sit. Latonya, did you know Fred used to
watch us through those windows and he said that the
glass made everything we Bells did look rosy?"

"I'm not surprised to hear it. Everything us Bells do is
rosy."

"Fred liked the way you kept our family straight. He
once told me that when he grew up and straightened
himself out, he hoped to marry you. You think you
would have ever married Fred?"

Latonya looked sad for a moment while she thought
this over. "It depends on how straight he got himself.

The letter of the law is not good enough for me. I have many goals to keep before I marry a man."

"What goals?"

She sipped her chocolate and gazed through the windows like they were bearing witness.

"My first one is to create a perfect wedding for Mama and then spend the rest of my life making Jack into the perfect husband that Mama deserves. My second goal is to master the French horn and then return to my dear sousa. Of course when school starts up in September, I will be striving for an *A* in every subject. I need to keep myself on an upward track toward doctorhood. What about you, Oren?"

"I guess in time I'll play the cornet as good as I did the trumpet. I think when we go back to school, I'll do a little better than ordinary. I'm better than a Dink because you make me do my homework, but I don't want the bother of being a doctor. I'll give you what help I can in shaping Jack up."

"I don't sense any passion in your goals, Oren. Isn't there anything that you want to do more than anything else?"

"I want to catch the person who murdered Fred."

"Catching murderers is policework."

"There are some the police never catch."

"Then make catching Fred's murderer a goal. In detective stories you start off by interviewing everybody who knew the victim. Let me give you a word of warning. Don't interview any of the neighborhood trash and stay away from crack houses."

"Those are the people and places that did Fred in. How do I get clues out of decent people and places?"

"That's for you to find out. I don't allow anybody in the family to put themselves in danger's way or talk to strangers or crooks. Good luck. I'm going to bed."

He decided to sit alone and stare into the windows while the clock struck midnight. He needed to take a magic thought from the windows. Mr. Sandman had told him that the little swirls and etches in the glass were actually pictures, done with lines of blue on the red. The blue lines were the Hebrews crossing the Red Sea. Crossing the Red Sea had been a miracle and a very difficult thing to do.

It wouldn't hurt to interview some of the decent people who knew Fred. Brenda had played inside the house next door when she shouldn't have. Granddaddy had spent a lot of time in the house next door when he needed a lonely place to drink his Red Rose wine. The thought came to Oren through the glass. What about people who were only half decent but not actually dangerous? Latonya couldn't object to him interviewing Aunt Grace. Aunt Grace was a friend of Fred's former foster mama's. What about the Goon Eye, who knew the same evil that Fred had known? When he had asked him about Dora and Tedfield Jones, the pores in his unwashed body had let off a smell of fear. Skyler Sims had split scared before he had to answer more questions. The crime was cold and getting colder. Oren would start his investigation first thing next morning.

Chapter 7

○　　○　　○

Oren listened to the talk around the breakfast table, biding his time until he could interview Granddaddy and Brenda.

"I do believe that Brenda's art has now hit the Picasso school straight on," Latonya said. Since Ms. Pugh had taken them through the art museum, Latonya felt the need to fit Brenda's pictures in a school. Oren looked at the one Brenda was working on.

"Maybe so."

"Of course I don't know anything about art," Mama said, "but the Picasso that I remember is a picture of a man with a big nose off center from his face. Brenda draws and paints ships and houses."

"That's right, Sarah," Granddaddy said. "You don't know anything about art. I can see that Brenda is painting in the Picasso-Sandman school. Picasso and Sandman make social comment in their pictures, and so does our Brenda. If you recall, the sad sinking and sunken ships she drew last year had their smokestacks off center. This here house she is painting has its chimney off center, and it looks like a fellow I knew years ago in Chicago. Definitely Brenda's art is in the Picasso school, although she needs work to bring it up to the Sandman school."

"I'm painting in the Brenda school," Brenda told them. "Mr. Sandman says my pictures are unique."

"What house is it that you're painting?" Latonya asked.

"Our house."

"Why is it so pink?" Oren asked in a kind voice, because Brenda looked to be a little riled by their comments.

"It's how our house looked to Fred when he was looking at us out the red windows."

Brenda knew that Fred watched them. Very interesting.

"Listen to me, Oren and Granddaddy," Latonya said. "Here is Mama's number at her office. Don't dial this number for any common emergency. If there is a fire, get Brenda, pup, and cat safely outside and call the fire department. Don't open the door to strangers."

"What kind of fools you take us for, Latonya Bell?" Granddaddy fumed. "Just get out of here and tend to your wedding business."

Brenda was dabbing in the impatiens. Oren slyly took himself beside her and pretended to be appreciating her artwork.

"Why are you specializing in buildings this year?"

"I'm very interested in buildings," Brenda said. "Mr. and Mrs. Sandman are going to take me on a downtown tour of Detroit buildings that are old and not being used right. Those kind have the best architecture."

"What makes you think that Fred watched us out of the red windows from the house next door when it was next door?"

"Because he told me."

"Fred told me so too," Granddaddy hollered from his living room chair.

Oren had always believed that he was the only one Fred confided in; but then of course Granddaddy had been kind of involved next door. The police had promised to keep secret what he had disclosed. Bill Bell forgot stuff and made up stuff, but, like he always said, even a clock that didn't work told the right time twice a day. Oren moved into the living room and pulled a stool up close to Granddaddy so Brenda couldn't listen.

"Don't breathe on me, Oren."

"As I understand it, Granddaddy, in the days when you frequented the house next door, you burned its trash on the first floor, while Fred ran errands for those who did business on the second floor. Is that correct?"

"That's correct. Fred was the delivery boy, and I was the human shredding machine. I burned what they told me in the fireplace. A bottle of wine seemed a fair wage for my sin at the time. The police pardoned me for what help I was able to give them, and I am not supposed to talk about it with uninvolved family members. Buzz off, Oren. You're disturbing the cat."

A subtle question that would unlock the crime; how could he put it?

"Granddaddy, who killed Fred?"

"I don't know. Fred always played one side of the hall against the other, and he was too smart mouth for his own good. I played my hand while drunk and stupid. Like a child, I saw no evil and spoke no evil. It was most likely his smart mouth that did Fred in."

"Why did Fred spend so much time up on the third floor of the house when his business was on the second?"

"He liked to fool around with the organ. Fred was a natural musician. The boy could have played Gabriel's horn if he hadn't had a devil on his back."

"I know another reason why Fred liked the top floor." Brenda stood in the doorway.

"What reason?"

"Fred didn't like to stay with any of the foster people that the social service people found for him. The house was his crib. The crack people didn't bother him on the top floor. He felt like the king of the world looking out of them red windows."

Fred had told him on many occasions that the house next door was his crib. It had been his crib before the crack people showed up. Like roaches, rats, or killer ants, they were nameless invaders. The house had been a simple haunted house when Fred had first taken it for his own.

"Oren, the puppy is yapping to go out. Do your duty by him."

Granddaddy's tone dismissed him. He took Tuffcity outside while Brenda returned to her painting. The morning sun was encouraging her impatiens, and the little flowers were busting out all over. Blue and Whitey were on the Fred Field shooting hoops. Those guys were so lucky. They had a summer ahead with no music lessons or math homework. Neither one had a little sister they were obliged to watch over. Neither one had actually been Fred's best friend, so they didn't have the same responsibility to find Fred's killer. But they had been his second-best friends, so they should help solve the murder. They might have noticed something that he had missed. Blue's brother was a cop. That had to be worth something.

"Hey, Oren, don't let your dog do his business on our basketball diamond," Whitey said.

"C'mon, man," Blue said. "Let's get to practice before the Beubiens come by."

"They won't come by till later," Oren said. "The Goon Eye says they like to wait till the big band shows up. The music gives them shooting power. Why don't we sit on my porch and have a little talk?"

"Sure. Latonya left some lemonade in the refrigerator."

When settled on the porch, Oren opened his line of questioning.

"I never told you guys because Fred told me not to tell, but he once invited me to join him in the crooked business that went on inside the house next door. I declined."

"He did the same to me." Blue finally said. "He wanted me to talk my brother into going along. I pretended I never heard him. Fred just pounded me on the shoulder and said we could still be brothers. I never told anybody, but Fred is dead and you brought it up, Oren."

"He never invited me in," Whitey said sadly.

"Who do you think killed Fred?" Oren asked.

"You said it. Latonya said it. It was the house that Spiro Spill built that done it. The house killed him, and now the house is gone. Leave it at that," Blue said.

This would never satisfy Oren.

Latonya had made up a rule for summer days because they blinked on and off so fast that some thought or event might slip by and be forgotten. At the end of each day they had to share events and experiences. Latonya began.

"Brenda will want to paint a picture of the Detroit Boat Club because it's so old and so grand. The location is also very good. The wedding will be at four o'clock at the church in the afternoon. The band concert will start at six o'clock on the island. The wedding reception will start before the band concert is over, but us musicians will be playing close enough, so we can change in and out of wedding finery and jog over from the bandstand to the club. The fireworks will start after dark and over- lap with the reception. We will have to keep strict to the schedule."

"Sounds like you are doing a bang-up job on planning the wedding," Oren said.

"Why are you buttering me up? I splatted a few notes

and I lost my temper and hollered at that Goon Eye character during band practice, and why is he hanging around and watching what we do? Never mind telling me. You think too slow, and I need to settle Brenda down for the night." She stomped off.

Mama was doing her homework in the kitchen. By the next night Jack would be hanging around and she wouldn't be ripe for serious interviewing. Mama didn't like to talk about how Fred got killed. He would have to be very careful in leading up to it.

"Mama, you never liked me hanging around with Fred."

She put her book down and looked thoughtful. "I had mixed feelings about your friendship with Fred. A mother likes her children to have friends with high goals and moral standards. *Influence* is the key word here."

"Aunt Grace always talks about influence when she is warning Dink and Dede to stay away from Latonya, Brenda, and me."

"That brings up the other side of influence," Mama admitted. "If a mother is fortunate enough to have bright and honest children, shouldn't she allow them to influence less fortunate children?"

"That's why you didn't back me off from hanging around with Fred?"

"I did like Fred and hoped that he would come around," Mama said. "But when he was killed, I was afraid for my children and started to believe that

Grace's thinking was the safer way. I'm glad that you brought this up, Oren."

"Mama, what bothers me is this. Everybody says that it was crack that killed Fred, or the house next door, or crime in the neighborhood. Granddaddy says that evil deeds are done by committees today. He may be right, but I need to put a face to Fred's killer."

"I do understand your need, but maybe crack killers don't have faces. Listen, Oren, while we're talking about our safety, we now have the means to move out of the neighborhood. I have my job, and Jack has paychecks from two good jobs. I say we should ponder the possibility of moving up and on."

"Consider, Mama. Brenda has her impatiens in full bloom, and Latonya and I have the Fred Band and Ball Field in full operation. Mr. Sandman is holding steady on Canfield Street. You know Ms. Pugh says we should stay and make where we are better."

Mama didn't answer. She just thoughtfully returned to her books, and Oren knew the interview was over. He went back to the dining room.

"Latonya, I want to talk to you about Fred."

"That's a painful subject. You remember how Ms. Pugh appointed me to be Fred's buddy in our seventh-grade homeroom class? I was supposed to keep Fred on the straight and narrow, and what did I do? I let him get murdered. If you choose to bring it up and rake it over and make me sorrowful and depressed, then feel free. Which Fred thing do you want to talk about?"

"You told me that I could only interview decent people. Latonya, you aren't to blame for Fred's murder. You were a good friend to him, so help me now. Who do you think killed Fred?"

"I'm not sure it was crack people who did it."

"Who, then?"

"Granddaddy says that Fred knew how to work both sides of the hall, and that's what did him in. In ways of working both sides of the hall, Fred was a master. He had more brains than your average adult trash. Something happened outside the regular wheeling and dealing inside the house."

"What?"

"How do I know? You're the detective here. I got a wedding to do, and it's no easy job. I'm going to bed."

"What about our bedtime chocolate?"

"Where is it written that I serve up chocolate to the likes of you each night? Brenda is down for the night. Granddaddy has gone to bed. You do likewise."

He stared bleakly into his reflection in the windows. He could interview Ms. Pugh and Mr. Shell. It was touchy. Ms. Pugh and Mr. Shell had held such high hopes for Fred. He didn't want to pain those good people unless it was essential. Latonya returned and set a mug of chocolate in front of him. She marched out of the room. He took a sip.

The next morning he sat in the kitchen alone, waiting for his math tutoring. When Ms. Pugh arrived, she had Mr. Shell with her. Two for one. He had to be quick before Mr. Shell went upstairs to his studio.

"Don't look so worried over those fractions, Oren. I'll help you solve them."

"I wasn't worried over the math, Ms. Pugh. I was thinking about Fred and who killed him."

There was a moment of silence. Oren recalled that Mr. Shell had once thought about adopting Fred. What if he had? Would Fred still be alive?

"I've been thinking about Fred a lot lately myself," Mr. Shell said. "I had a talk with him the day before he was killed. I told him that he had a rare, God-given talent. I had said that to him before, but this time he seemed to listen. I knew that I couldn't move him out of that wreck next door, but I told him I could arrange for him to study with a man who plays with the Detroit Symphony Orchestra. He said he'd think about it. I thought I'd made a major breakthrough with the kid. That was the last time I ever talked with him."

"Yesterday I was thinking about a book report that Fred handed in last year," Ms. Pugh said. "At the beginning of the year he had no interest in words or books, but he was quick to learn. The last report he handed in was on *Moby Dick*. His paper said simply, '*Moby Dick* is a how-to book on whaling. If a reader wants to go after a whale, this book tells them all they need to know.' I said to him, "Fred, *Moby Dick* is a much more than a whaling story." He said, "Oh yeah, that man-against-nature stuff." Then he proceeded to touch on all of the great symbolic points in the story. Fred was a remarkable boy. Very deep."

Oren knew that Fred had picked up the great symbolic points out of Brenda's Classics Illustrated *Moby Dick* comic book.

"Who do you think killed Fred?" he asked.

They both thought this over. Finally Ms. Pugh said, "There is such an underculture in the city. Fred never joined a gang. The gangs might have resented a loner like Fred, who had connections to important crime people."

"I think Pat is right," Mr. Shell said. "Fred wasn't black, he wasn't white, and he wasn't Oriental. He claimed to be an American Indian, but whatever he was, he looked different and acted different. He also had a big mouth. Neighborhood gangs don't like different kids with big mouths."

Mr. Shell went upstairs, and Ms. Pugh sat down next to Oren and started checking his math.

So they both thought gangs killed Fred, but gangs didn't have one face Oren could see and know.

Oren and Wesley were setting up for band practice. As soon as he was done, Oren said, "Wesley, who do you think killed Fred?"

She looked down at her music stand. "I think a bad person killed Fred."

"Would a bad person need a reason?"

"Yes. A bad reason."

What would provoke a bad person to kill? Fred's mouth had respected the boss trash he worked for in the house next door. He was more inclined to wise off to the small-time trash hanging around the fringes of his diverse activities. Oren took his cornet out of its case and looked at his reflection in the bell. He looked like a worried face in a Picasso painting. Tomorrow he would have to interview the half-decents. Aunt Grace might not add any new information, but she wouldn't mind talking. She had said many times it was Fred's fault that he had gotten himself killed. Dink might have picked up a little information from the overflow of Aunt Grace's mouth. The Goon Eye imagined himself to be a friend of Fred's. The half-decents, without meaning to, just might give him the clue he needed.

Chapter 8

○　　○　　○

"Get serious, people," Latonya said. "We need to make decisions on who is to be cast in what role for the big day."

"I do have a few ideas of my own to contribute," Aunt Grace said.

"Then keep them to yourself, Grace," Granddaddy said. "Go ahead, Latonya."

"First off, Mama, who do you want to be your maid of honor?"

"I would be pleased to have Latonya be my maid of honor, and Brenda for my junior maid of honor," Mama said. "And I have a dear friend from my old J. L. Hudson days who would like to be included."

"Fair enough," Latonya allowed.

"My daughter, Dede, had just better be marching down that aisle," Aunt Grace said. "Dede has always been more dependable than Brenda, and she is in better mental health."

"Now, Jack"—Latonya passed over Aunt Grace— "you get to pick a best man."

"I pick Oren for my best man. I have a friend from my university days who I would like included."

"My son, Dooley, had just better be standing up front," Aunt Grace said.

"Grace, you're trying to make a circus out of our wedding," Granddaddy said.

Oren admired the way that Latonya was keeping her calm. Most wedding planners didn't have to contend with Aunt Grace.

"We do need Dink to put the runner down for the bride and bridesmaids to walk on. Mr. Shell and Ms. Pugh are arranging the music. Wesley is keeping the wedding book. Dede can hold the pen. The penholder is important." Latonya paused and looked thoughtful. "If Aunt Grace will consent to give a special reading before the ceremony begins, it would be lovely."

Mama spoke up. "I would like Bill Bell to give me away."

"That is totally inappropriate, Sarah," Aunt Grace said. "Bill Bell is only your drunken ex-father-in-law, the father to the scum of the earth, your ex-husband."

Oren expected Granddaddy to jump right in, but he looked kind of crushed. Aunt Grace had finally found a way to put him down.

"Grace Bell, you watch your mouth when you talk about our father," Jack said.

"He'll never make it down that long aisle," Aunt Grace kept on. "His limbs tremble when he walks, and his lungs wheeze."

"It is my duty and pleasure to give Sarah away to Jack."

"Thank you, Dad," Mama said.

"Then so be it," Latonya said. "Now we will get to the flowers."

"No picking my impatiens." Brenda stopped painting on her picture and put a finger in the air.

"Don't worry, Miss," Latonya said. "Wesley's mother loves to arrange flowers. She is rising early on the morning of the wedding and going to the Farmer's Market to make a beautiful selection. I think we've accomplished quite a bit here this morning, people. Now let's get out there and be at our business for the day."

"If you are all going over to play on your junk pile on Canfield Street, I'll be by later in the afternoon in my truck to take you to music lessons," Aunt Grace said.

"You didn't write that letter to the mayor, did you, Aunt Grace?" Oren said.

"I sure did. It's the business of every concerned citizen to clean up our city."

Aunt Grace marched upstairs. She liked to vacuum the white shaggy carpeting in the upstairs music studio before Mr. Shell arrived. She had lived upstairs the year before and had been the one to order the carpeting from the store, although Mama made the payments on it.

"Latonya, you take Brenda to the art project, and I'll come by later. I think I'll take time to have a little talk with Aunt Grace."

Latonya gave him a wink.

○

Aunt Grace handed him a bottle of water and a rag.

"These windows haven't been washed since I moved out. You climb up on that stepladder and do the ones at the side of the fireplace. Get busy, now. Make those panes shine."

What a detective didn't have to do to get information. "Aunt Grace, I've been noticing that your friend Dora Dillworthy has quite a few children. Sometimes they come over and play by our artwork."

"Dora tells them to stay away from that junk, but children don't listen. It's not as if those children belong to her in the true sense of being born to her, so the poor woman can't be expected to be responsible for their actions."

"How do they belong to her?" Oren said very cool, like he didn't know.

"Dora's children come and go. She's a foster mother by trade and the most Christian of women. She takes troublemakers and strays that the social services can't place anywhere else. Dora has the good intentions of a saint."

Oren cleaned and polished the window to Aunt Grace's satisfaction. He put on his probing face and started on the second window. "I seem to remember that Mrs. Dillworthy was a foster mama to Fred Lightfoot."

"Oh, Lordy, what a trial that boy was for the poor woman. Dora was an expert on dealing with unruly rejects, but Fred came straight from the devil with his tricking ways. He shocked her and he mocked her. He didn't come home to sleep in the bed assigned to him. Dora is too refined to go into places of ill repute and rescue run-offs. I don't know what she would have done if she hadn't had her good friend Tedfield Jones in control of discipline. Many the times she had to send Teddy to fetch Fred out of the house next door. It took a heavy hand to handle Fred. You did a nice job on those windows, now go check on Dooley. I don't want him in that dirty Fred Field. Dooley is a good boy, but sometimes he forgets what his mother tells him."

Dink was sitting in the Bell kitchen staring at the wall. It was possible that he was thinking about something, but Oren doubted it. No need to be subtle when questioning Dink.

"Dink." He waved a hand in front of the kid's face.

"Does my mother want me?"

"She just wants me to check on you. I'm checking. Dink, is Tedfield Jones Dora Dillworthy's man?"

"Sure he is. He's a common-law husband to her."

"Then, why is he living in the house next door to her?"

"That's easy. He killed one of her foster children a few years back. It was an accident, and my mother says he was provoked into doing it. He mighta been a little drugged up at the time. He didn't spend much time in jail over it, but the Social Services won't give Dora any foster children to keep if Teddy lives with her. Dora thinks Teddy learned his lesson. He even goes to church with her now."

Oren thought this over. Teddy Jones moved right into the vacant house next door to Dora, and the Social Services Department didn't pick up on it. No system knew what the neighborhood knew. Social Services was overworked and understaffed. Blue and Whitey suspected Teddy's house of being a crack house, but every empty house bore that suspicion. Teddy could just be living in an empty city house. Lots of people did. Aunt Grace had said that Tedfield Jones had a heavy hand when provoked, but Fred had been strong and cunning. Fred would have killed Teddy if they'd had some kind of a scuffle.

Dink was looking at him like he expected a reward for the information. Actually Dink had done good.

"Dink, I'm going outside to shoot a few hoops. If you stand back and keep the dust off your body, you can come and watch."

"Your talk with Aunt Grace must have swayed her to our side," Latonya said. "How come she's letting Dink and Dede come over here to Canfield Street?"

"Because she wants to nap all afternoon. She's only allowing them to watch."

"Those two are so interested in Mr. Sandman's art that Aunt Grace may stop writing to the mayor."

"Fat chance."

"Did you see what he made from the door that was on the haunted house? The Detroit Institute of Art has asked him if they can put it on exhibit. Art shows, band concerts, athletic contests—our neighborhood is flying high into the twenty-first century."

"Don't you want to know how my investigation's going?"

"How's the investigation going?"

He looked around. Brenda had at least twenty children painting and weeding around the flowers. Tuffcity was going from friendly hand to friendly hand to be petted. There were grown people cutting the grass and making little parks for Mr. Sandman's sculptures.

"There's too many ears around, but I'll tell you tonight."

"Mama and Jack are going on a double date with Mr. Shell and Ms. Pugh; but Wesley's staying over, and Brenda will want to stay up late. Granddaddy will be sleeping with one ear open in his chair."

"Wesley's been tested and trusted. Granddaddy's been sober for a time. The more brains the better, and Brenda is our best brain. I can lay out what I have discovered and deducted."

When Aunt Grace picked them up, her nap had put her in top form. She stood shoulder to shoulder with Dora Dillworthy and surveyed their work.

"I am mystified by all this. I don't understand it," Dora said.

"What's to understand about junk?" Aunt Grace said. "This artist man is dangerous. He's changing the face of the neighborhood. People from all over are coming to view this stuff. We have to do something."

"Isn't changing the face of the neighborhood good, Mama?" Dede said.

"There's a right and a wrong way to do everything, Dede child. Oren and Latonya, you walk Tuffcity home. I don't want dog hair in my truck."

Tuffcity heeled behind them like a good dog. They walked home in silence, but Oren could feel Latonya thinking about Fred's murder. It was a twin thing they had. She was sharing the passion of his goal.

Chapter 9

○   ○   ○

Early evening was the time for baseball. Grand-daddy called them the boys of summer, even though Latonya was their hardest hitter and Wesley was the best fast-ball pitcher. Jack supplied balls and bats. Kids from both sides of Woodward were coming over to have a turn at bat or to sit and cheer.

The Goon Eye's men were now helping to enforce the rules. The Goon Eye coached one team, and Oren coached the other.

"The Goon Eye calls his team the Pistols," Blue said. "We need a tough name for our team."

"The Tuffcity Beagles, after our pup," Brenda suggested.

"Not tough enough," Blue said.

"How about the Pit Bulls?" Whitey said.

"How about the Fourth Street Fools?" Granddaddy said.

"If Wesley and I weren't on the team, that might work," Latonya said.

"We'll call ourselves the Stooges," Oren said. "And we will be the best."

"Oren, I wanna play ball," Dink said. "My mother gave me permission. She bought me a mitt."

"We need you to be water boy, Dink."

"You got Brenda and Dede for water boys."

"You can play on the Goon Eye's team."

"The Goon Eye says he'll take me if Latonya plays with the Pistols."

"All right, Dink. You can be on our team. Take your mitt out in left field and try to look like a Stooge."

The Fred Field didn't have lights, so it closed at sundown. When Jack and Mr. Shell told them all that game time was over, both teams disbanded and drifted off in good spirits. Blue and Whitey had permission to sleep over. The Goon Eye hung back, too, a wistful expression on his moon face, like he wished he could stay but knew he'd never be asked.

Oren was designated to get permission from Jack because he knew how to direct and control Jack better than Latonya. Latonya was approaching Mama on the same issue. Jack was in the bathroom shaving for his date.

"Jack, I'd like to ask your opinion on something."

"Shoot."

"What?"

"Go ahead and talk."

Why would a man say "Shoot" when he meant "Talk"? "Listen, Jack, Blue, and Whitey have been invited to stay over. I told them they could stay in the upstairs music flat. It's fine with Mama. I knew it would be fine with you. What do you think?"

"It's fine with me, Oren."

"Plenty of room up there. I also told Skyler Sims he could stay over. The more the better, I always say."

"Who is Skyler Sims?"

"To some he is known as the Goon Eye."

"Absolutely not. The kid has a police record and he sleeps in doorways."

"The Goon Eye's trying to get himself off drugs. Latonya and Brenda believe that he's growing from half decent to decent. That's growth, Jack."

"The Goon Eye was never half decent. Your mother and I expect you to associate with better young people than the likes of him."

"Mama says that it's the duty of her children to rub some of their goodness off on the less fortunate. We're not allowed to think like Aunt Grace in this house."

"Sarah did say something like that. I don't want to think like Grace. How about your grandfather? He's the senior Bell in residence tonight. What does Bill say?"

"Granddaddy says anybody who's not Aunt Grace is welcome."

"I'll talk it over with your mother."

By the time Jack and Mama were spiffed up for their dinner and concert, a compromise had been worked out. Mr. Shell was going to return after the concert and sleep upstairs with Blue, Whitey, and the Goon Eye. The Goon Eye had been waiting on the porch, and he was beside himself when he was let inside. He was going to spend the night with decent people and sleep on white, shaggy carpeting.

They sat around the dining room table under the red eyes. Before Oren could start his investigation, invitations to the wedding had to be written and sent off. Latonya had decided on postcards. She had composed the message and made up a guest list.

"I don't write so good, Latonya," the Goon Eye admitted. "Brenda says I can color pictures while you all are writing."

"You can also lick the stamps," Latonya said.

"Don't expect me to write any invitations or lick any stamps, Latonya," Granddaddy said. "And no loud partying from you folks. I'm going to bed. All that Fred Field fresh air got to me."

It was exactly midnight when the invitations were done. Latonya and Wesley went out to the kitchen to heat up some hot chocolate. The Friends of Fred sat around the table, their faces glowing a mysterious color from the overhead light and the red-glass windows. Tuffcity was sleeping on the floor, and they could hear Granddaddy snoring down the hall. It was a comforting sound.

"I think the time has come for us to talk about Fred's murder," Oren said.

"Under the eyes of the house that murdered him?" Whitey said.

"What hasn't been already said about it?" Blue asked.

"Who did it and why," Oren said.

Latonya and Wesley returned with the cookies and chocolate. They solemnly took their seats. The overhead lamp gave a frantic flicker and went out.

There was a long moment when nobody dared say a word.

"The eyes are blinking at me," Whitey finally said.

"The windows catch the headlights from passing cars," Latonya said. She lit a candle and placed it in the middle of the table.

"See our shadows on the wall," Brenda said. "A gathering of giants."

The time had come to talk about the dark and evil matters that went on in the night.

"Brenda, why doesn't your ghost hang around anymore?" Blue asked. "Spiro might be very useful in solving a case like this."

"I let Spiro go because I don't need him now."

"Would he come back if you needed him?"

"I don't think so. Spiro Spill has gone over and through the rainbow and can't return."

"How 'bout Fred's ghost?" the Goon Eye wanted to know. "He must want his own murder to be solved."

"I don't think so," Latonya said. "Fred didn't believe in ghosts. I know that for a fact. What do you say, Brenda?"

"Fred didn't and doesn't believe in ghosts, so he can't be one."

"Then we'll have to do it on our own," Oren said. "You don't have any knowledge of murders, do you,

Wesley? I don't suppose you have that many in the 'burbs."

"No, we don't have as many, but we read and talk about them a lot. It was said that Fred's murder was drug related. It's hard to say which drug pusher pulled the trigger."

"It wasn't no trigger," the Goon Eye said. "Fred was killed with a blunt instrument to the back of his head."

All attention was on the Goon Eye. Oren knew that the police hadn't released that information to the news.

"Wasn't totally what you would call drug related either. Was it, Goon Eye?" Oren said.

"Not totally. Look, you guys. I like hanging out with you good citizens, but I'm scared."

They were all so quiet, you could hear the clock tick. In candlelight they watched the juices going berserk inside the Goon Eye.

"You were there, weren't you?" Oren said.

The Goon Eye opened his mouth, but words refused to come out.

Brenda broke the silence. "Skyler, we are a secret society of friends. We tell ghost stories. We're under the protection of the red eyes. The more horrible the story you make up, the better for us to hear it. Our stories never go outside this room. It's your turn to tell one. Your story is safe with us. Tell us, Skyler."

Another long quiet. Latonya took the Goon Eye's shaking hand and held it. "Go on, Skyler, tell your story."

He started to talk—slow and mumbling at first.

"Once upon a time there were two boys. One was real smart and the other was kind of stupid, but they were both foster boys and liked each other. Foster boys are a cut below orphan boys, because orphans sometimes get adopted, but fosters never do. In my story I'll call the smart boy Sly and the stupid boy Dim. Sly didn't want parents. It was no trick for him to get himself friends and money. Some of the friends and money he acquired were honest and some not. Sly knew how to talk down to kings and up to beggars. Sometimes he went inside churches just to listen to the music. Sly was very musical. It was nothing for Sly to read the words in books and the notes in music. Dim couldn't read books or music, or make good friends or honest money, but he sure admired the way that Sly could do those things. Dim mostly got together with others like himself and became a leader of losers, but Sly told him he could do better. "Come along with me," Sly said. "I will let you be my assistant."

The Goon Eye stopped, and they all waited. Wesley took his other hand.

"Go on with the story, Skyler," Brenda whispered. "We are your friends and we love you. We are the giants on the wall."

Finally the Goon Eye gave a sigh that nearly put out the candle.

"Sly lived in a grand mansion house that had long ago been deserted by honest people. The house was no common crack house. There was what Sly called diverse business going on downstairs and upstairs. On two floors there was wheeling and dealing, but way up on top of the house there was a special place that Sly called his penthouse. He could look out on the city through rosy-colored glass. There was a big old musical instrument for him to play on. There were safe and hidden corners for him to sleep in, but Sly was still a kid and had to report in to foster mamas. Most of his foster mamas had locked their doors to him when he didn't make it home by their bedtime. Sly liked it that way, but one day he got a big old foster mama who was out to do her job right. She had a mean old man to send after Sly if he didn't come home by the time she said. The foster mama and daddy knew where Sly hung out, but most times the foster daddy was scared to go inside the house. The people who did business on the second floor were not his gang. They'd 'ave wiped out that small-time foster daddy if he came inside. Sly said the house was protecting his rights. One night the house was empty except for the two boys on the top floor. Sly was working on the organ by the light of a candle. He said he thought there was a dead mouse up one of its pipes. That Sly could fix anything. Dim, he was sleeping on his blanket back in the eaves and shadows of the room."

There was another long silence, broken only by Granddaddy's ungodly snores. They were all afraid of what was coming next. Oren knew it was his place to encourage the witness.

"I guess the foster daddy wasn't afraid to come inside the house when he saw it was empty of the gang."

"No, he wasn't afraid," the Goon Eye went on. "He

was maybe doped or drunk. While Sly was working on the big organ and Dim was sleeping on his blanket way back in the shadows, feet came stamping up the stairs. Sly didn't take the bother to turn around when the door opened. He knew who it was and he didn't care. He just kept at fixing his organ. The foster daddy came in the door and he was bull mad. His woman had made him come after Sly. He had a lead pipe in his hand. Most times he used the pipe to hit on the arms and legs of kids when they refused to do what he said. He told that boy to git himself home on the double. Sly kept working. The man told him to turn around. He said, "Look me in the eye when I talks to you, you little shit." Sly still didn't turn around, but he said the house was his crib and he wasn't ever going back to his foster mama's house. He told the man to get lost or he would sic the house on him. The man was worked up to a full rage. He took that lead pipe and hit Sly over the back of his head until he was dead. The man looked at what he had done. Dim was in the corner of the room on his blanket, but the man never saw him. The man took Sly's body and went off downstairs. The candle by the organ went out, and Dim didn't see no more. What the man did was put Sly's body in one of the second-floor rooms, so as the police would think the people who did business in the house killed the kid. That's the end of my story."

It was so quiet, even Granddaddy's snoring had stopped. They studied the giants on the wall and their reflections in the panes of the windows. Finally Latonya said, "Why didn't Dim go to the police?"

"He was stupid, not crazy. The man had killed a kid before and didn't do much jail time for it. Dim wanted Sly's killer to be put away, but the police weren't going to believe a dumb kid with a record. Dim don't want that old foster daddy to come after him with a lead pipe."

"Sly wouldn't expect Dim to go to the police," Oren said. His insides were kicking up worse than the time when he had eaten the old potato salad, but the overwhelming feeling was sadness. He had imagined that Fred was murdered by a big-time, international crime boss, but his friend had been done in by a common little neighborhood punk.

"Why didn't Dim tell the foster mama? Your story didn't make her out to be a bad woman," Wesley said.

"She weren't no bad woman. She knew her man was mean, but she just didn't want to believe he was a killer. It's easy for a woman to get foster children but not so easy to get a good man. That lady will keep giving Sly's killer one more chance until somebody gives her full proof."

"You guys, I don't believe what the Goon Eye is telling us is a made-up story," Whitey said wisely.

"Thank you, Whitey," Blue said. "When a kid thinks with his kidney instead of his brain, it takes a while for him to figure things out. My brother says, when there's a killing, the police first suspect a member of the victim's family. I guess Dora and Tedfield were Fred's family, but Dora didn't tell them nothin' about sending Teddy after Fred. Most likely Teddy told her that when he arrived, there were drug-business people in the house. She wouldn't expect him to go inside if he said that."

"Whatever excuses went on between Dora and Tedfield, we were Fred's real family," Latonya said. "I agree that we shouldn't tell anybody until we have proof. Mama and Jack would go to the police. We need to commit ourselves here tonight to getting a full confession from the killer. We have to be very careful, because Brenda here is just a child."

"I am not."

The story the Goon Eye had told them was heavy stuff, but Oren felt more settled. He had all his friends working together. Latonya continued, "We need to put a time limit on our silence. If we can't put Teddy away before school starts in September, we'll go to the police."

"That's plenty of time. Step by step we'll drive Tedfield Jones crazy until he gives up and confesses," Brenda said.

"Excellent." Brenda had given Oren the plan. "Blue, Whitey, remember how Fred and the Three Stooges used to drive our teachers crazy before Ms. Pugh showed up and made us stop?"

"We retired three of 'em in the fifth grade, and five in the sixth grade," Blue remembered with a dirty laugh.

"It was five in the fifth grade and nine in the sixth grade," Whitey said.

"That's the way Fred would want us to do it. We can't have a big stir before the wedding. The operation has to be undercover." Oren looked at the determined faces around the table for approval.

"You heard my brother," Latonya said. "Let's take an oath on it."

"I am the oathmaker," Brenda said.

Tuffcity gave his welcoming bark. Latonya went to the window. "Mama, Jack, and Mr. Shell are home. Start the oath and make it short."

"You sure your grandfather is asleep?" Wesley said. "I haven't heard him snore for a while."

"He's dead to the world when he quits snoring," Oren said. "Brenda, hurry."

The gathering of giants around the table and on the wall clasped hands.

"By our word not our blood, under the Red Windows, who saw Fred murdered, we take this oath," Brenda said. "We the Friends of Fred hereby dedicate our lives to driving that scum, Tedfield Jones, crazy before school starts in September. Even if tortured, we refuse to tell what we are about to family or cops, because it might get Skyler hurt or worse."

"I don't wanna get hurt," the Goon Eye said, "but no matter what happens, I got peace of mind. I told my story to Fred's friends, who are now my friends too."

Mama was pleased to see them enjoying one another's company, but Jack said, "Why is it so dark? I put fresh light bulbs in the kitchen cupboard yesterday. I told Oren and Latonya. Why don't they listen to me?"

"They were most likely telling ghost stories," Mama

said. "Blue, Whitey, Skyler, Mr. Shell is waiting for you upstairs. You all have a nice sleep-in."

That night the old house on the corner of Fourth and Hancock Street settled down with the Friends of Fred sleeping tightly in its rooms.

Chapter 10

○   ○   ○

"Tomorrow's the wedding! We have a full day ahead, Oren," Latonya said.

"Granddaddy, Jack, and me picked up our white suits. You women have your dresses. The church and The Detroit Boat Club are ready and waiting for us. What's left?"

"Plenty. You're such an innocent as to all the particulars that go into a perfect wedding. Your assignment is to care for Brenda while I carry out final details. You do remember that we have our last band rehearsal at half past noon?"

"Mr. Shell's reminded us so many times that his voice is nearly gone."

"Orchestrating and carrying out a perfect concert is very stressful. Then at three o'clock Jack and Mama are taking us to look at a new apartment. We surely don't need that aggravation."

"What's your opinion?"

"I think we should humor Mama and Jack. Looking at apartments has become the loving and social thing they do together. It's harmless enough. After the wedding we'll move Jack upstairs and get on with our lives."

How could a girl who got all *A*'s in school be so dumb? Jack was not going to be satisfied with being moved upstairs. Mama had assured Oren that looking for a new home was a process that could go on for months or even years, but you never knew when the one that satisfied them would come along. Still, him and Latonya and Brenda could point out how today's place wouldn't do.

"Pay attention, Oren. After band practice and the apartment we have Aunt Grace's rehearsal dinner and then the rehearsal at the church."

Latonya finally left. He cleaned up the breakfast dishes.

"Granddaddy, I need to take Brenda to the art project. Will you take care of Tuffcity?"

"No. It tires me to let him in and let him out. I need to save my legs for the big march down the center aisle tomorrow. I'll watch Skid."

"Aren't you going to walk down the aisle tonight at the rehearsal?"

"No. Like I said, I need to save my legs."

Oren thought it was a little risky for Granddaddy not to test his legs at least once. Still, he had blown true on his trumpet when his lip was gone. He might be able to walk Mama down the aisle one time. It was a little early to start worrying over that one. Brenda was ready to go, so he leashed the pup, and they took off.

The Goon Eye was busy working on the back of the

house when they arrived. He had painted in two orange figures with round heads, box bodies, and no legs. The figures were floating up toward Brenda's sun.

"Those are foster boys without anchors. Aren't they, Skyler?" Brenda said.

"You called it, little Brenda," the Goon Eye said.

She sure had an eye for art. Oren wondered which orange figure was Fred and which one was Skyler. Probably Brenda knew.

"Listen to me," the Goon Eye said. "I have an idea about what we were talking about the night you invited me to stay over."

Oren and Brenda stayed silent. They had been waiting for the subject to rise up again. The Goon Eye looked around. It was early, and the street was quiet. Mr. Sandman had gone inside to breakfast.

"I'm not sixteen yet," he finally said.

"You could have fooled me," Oren said. "You have a pretty good beard, and the Social Services people have given up looking for you."

"I've had face and body hair for a while, but I do sort of keep track of my years. I think I still might be at fifteen. I could turn myself in to the Social Services and ask them to see if Dora would take me back. That way I could look out for the children she has staying with her now. She always lets the oldest take care of the younger ones."

"Teddy might have told her what you told us," Oren said.

"No. Teddy thinks having a respectable woman puts

him a cut above the rest of the dope heads. He don't
want Dora to know about it. Besides, she's a big, strong
lady and she might kill him if she knew. Being scared of
Dora and the cops makes him likely to hurt a kid again. I
need to keep an eye on Tedfield Jones while you all get
your plan moving. I'm a Friend of Fred now, too, ya
know."

"You sleeping in the same house with Teddy sounds
perilous to me," Oren said. "Maybe we should go to the
police."

"Listen, you guys," Brenda said. "We took an oath.
What we need to do is get a plan working right now. I
have one."

They both gave her their full attention.

"Does Teddy know that I talk to ghosts and flowers?"
she asked rather proudly.

"It's common knowledge around the neighborhood,
Brenda," Oren admitted.

"Teddy especially knows it," the Goon Eye said. "He
brags that way back he come from Haitian stock, people
who knew all about ghosts. Once I heard him telling
Dora that the little Bell girl had powers; but Brenda, you
told us you don't have a ghost now and you said Fred
won't take the bother to haunt."

"Old Teddy doesn't know that. We can make up a Fred
ghost to haunt him, one that's worse than a real one.
You sure Teddy never saw you, Skyler?"

"Never. There was only a candle burning by the organ, and I was a pile of rags in a far corner. He never
even looked in my direction."

"Then as far as he knows, it's only the red windows that saw him do it," Oren said.

"That's the first message that we send him," Brenda said.

"How?" The Goon Eye asked.

"We might be able to work it into the art project," Brenda said.

"If we paint it on the side of a house, he'll suspect we're involved," Oren pointed out.

"No." Brenda turned. "On that tree by where his car is parked. Skyler, go to Mr. Sandman's supply shed and bring me some chalk. Red if there is any."

"Teddy'll see us do it," Oren said.

"He won't be up and out on the world for hours," the Goon Eye said.

The tree had cast-off toys draped on its branches and a doll with a cracked head sitting in a broken doll bed at its base. Brenda took a slate with alphabet letters around its frame, the kind that come off and stick where you put them. She spelled THE WINDOWS SAW. She placed the slate inside the open arms of the doll. The grim message didn't stand out plain for the world to see, but a guilty man unlocking the door of his car would surely note it.

"Here's the red chalk."

"You go draw two big red windows to the side of our art house, below my sun and over your falling boys."

"They'll be rained off before the day is over. There's already a fine mist in the air," Oren said.

"That's what we want. Now he sees them, then he

doesn't. Draw them quick. Just two big squares. Nothing fancy."

Oren marveled at Brenda's brain.

After drawing the windows Oren and the Goon Eye raked a yard and swept the street. Brenda looked for weeds in her flowers. Tuffcity barked at the Sandmans' door. Susan Sandman always had a friendly pat and a little food for him. When it was time for them to leave, the houses at the end of the street still had not come awake. Brenda eyed a broken cookie jar of many colors lying by the sidewalk on the grass, waiting to make an artistic statement. She put the pieces together so that they said FRED, and then she fitted them around the street sign.

The three Friends of Fred and their dog walked home.

The Goon Eye said, "I like your plan, Brenda, but I'm still going to turn myself in to Dora."

The last band rehearsal would have gone better if Mr. Shell had kept their feet solid on the Fred Field. They had been performing *The 1812 Overture* really well, but he decided that they should march through the neighborhood and spread the sound around. Oren, Latonya, Dink, and Wesley had been suited up in the official Northwestern Band uniforms so that they would blend in. The band marched smartly all the way to Woodward Avenue, children and a few winos falling in step behind. *The 1812 Overture* wasn't up to standard, because it was a windy day and the music kept blowing off the little stands attached to their instruments. Mr. Shell kept hollering words that they couldn't hear. He should have been saving his voice for the Big Day. Wesley was getting very good on her cymbals.

At three o'clock sharp they were back home to look at an apartment.

"You want to go with us, Bill?" Jack asked.

"No. I need to save my legs for the Big Day."

The apartment was downtown in a complex on the new river area. Jack sounded like a tour guide.

"These buildings once housed a famous Detroit drug company. Miracle medicines were born here. Latonya and Brenda, notice the nineteenth-century architecture. Sarah, there's an excellent security system and we're close to the university, and not far from where we'll both be working. How about that bike and jogging path, and that playground area? Cool breezes off the river while we play. What a life, huh?"

Jack had a key to the apartment.

"See, Brenda, there's a space for you to plant flowers in front." The space was too small for Brenda's impatiens.

They followed him inside. The walls were made out of the old brick from the drug company.

"Sarah, your red windows would look beautiful hanging on that brick."

Mama nodded.

"Look, Latonya," he pointed out. "An automatic dishwasher, new stove, new refrigerator."

"The kitchen is too small to sit down in. Three thin people standing close together is all it will hold."

"We'll eat in the dining room," Jack said.

Oren knew what his sister was thinking. Their big round table was a valuable antique that Latonya and Mama had found at the Salvation Army store. This dining room was too narrow for a big table. No space for company dinners or a meeting of the Friends of Fred.

Jack took them upstairs to look at the bedrooms. There was one on the second level that he thought would be nice for Mama and him, and two on a third level. There was a view of the river from one of the third-level bedrooms. Jack said Oren might have that one for his own, because Latonya and Brenda would need the larger one that faced the parking lot.

"Where would Granddaddy sleep?" Oren asked.

"Bill doesn't like stairs. He would have a comfortable sofa bed in the living room and of course his favorite chair. What do you think about the apartment as a whole?" Jack looked at them hopefully.

"It's nice enough for some people, but not for us," Latonya said kindly.

"It's beautiful, but I think the rent is too high," Mama said.

"Do they allow dogs and cats?" Brenda asked.

"They'd allow Skid, and we could find a good home for Tuffcity," Jack offered.

"It won't do," Brenda said.

That was about it for Jack's apartment. Oren felt a little sorry for him.

By six o'clock they were all dressed. They were just leaving when the phone rang, and they held on while

Latonya answered. When she returned, Oren could tell something was wrong. Of course something had to fall through.

"Aunt Grace says she is so mad at them, but Carl's Chop House won't accept her credit. She only has half the money to pay the bill. She is sorry."

"I told you so. I told you so. I told you so," Granddaddy said.

"Mama, I am talking about a host of people. Aunt Grace went and invited more than who are in the wedding party and she ordered up steak and lobster for one and all. I didn't say she couldn't, because I thought she was paying. I spent every last cent of the money you allowed me for the wedding. What are we going to do?" Latonya wailed.

"Bill was right," Jack said. "We shouldn't have involved Grace in the wedding. We'll have to put the tab on my credit card."

Oren could tell that Mama didn't like that idea much. She and Jack had decided that she would be the one to pay the bills after they were married. Credit cards made Mama nervous.

"We'll take part from our honeymoon money," Mama said.

"Part?" Granddaddy laughed out loud. "When Grace and her friends get through pigging out, you won't have enough honeymoon money left for that three-day cruise. You and Jack will be swimming home."

"We'll figure something out," Mama said. "Grace is family, Bill. Back when I didn't have bread to put on the table for the children, she shared what she had. Grace and I went through hard times together when there was nobody else." Mama's chin was up.

Granddaddy mumbled something under his breath to Jack, but neither one of them said another word.

The ride to the restaurant was quiet. Latonya had taken all of the guilt for Aunt Grace's cheapness on herself. When they got to the restaurant, Aunt Grace was in a party mood and playing hostess-with-the-mostest. She introduced Mama and Jack to all the people they didn't know. Oren heard her take Mama aside and tell her that it was her obligation as a wife to spend as much of Jack's money as she could. From Aunt Grace's view Granddaddy was a freeloader because he wasn't paying for any of the rehearsal dinner. The thing that really blew Oren's mind was that Aunt Grace had invited Dora Dillworthy and Tedfield Jones. Of course Dora was Aunt Grace's friend, and neither lady knew what the Friends of Fred knew. The thing about Tedfield Jones, he looked to be common and harmless. He wasn't a big man. A person who didn't know might classify Teddy to be more squirrel than weasel.

"Latonya," Oren took her aside, "do you think we could call a meeting of the Friends of Fred before dinner is served up? Could we gather out behind the restaurant without causing any notice?"

"I'm not eating any steak and lobster. I want to take my lobster home and give it some love," Brenda said.

"Two pets is all we allow in this family, Miss Brenda. Oren, Aunt Grace wouldn't let me invite Blue and Whitey to the rehearsal dinner. I didn't even try for poor Skyler. We're lucky that she let us invite Wesley and her family."

"Fetch Wesley, and we'll clue the rest in later."

They met inside the van. Oren told them about Brenda's idea to haunt Teddy Jones with a made-up ghost.

"I love it," Wesley said. "Where do all your great ideas come from, Brenda?"

"They just keep coming. I wonder what happens to the ones I don't say out loud or put into action. Where do those ideas go, Latonya?"

"I don't know, but it would distress Mama if she thought that you had another ghost. She would take you to a head doctor, and that would cost money."

"Mama's attention will be taken up with honeymooning for the next few days," Oren said.

"The ghost idea has possibilities," Latonya allowed. "What we need to do is convince Aunt Grace that Fred is back. She'd get the information to Teddy Jones quick enough."

"I'll give her the info," Oren said. "Wesley, you back us up."

"What do I do?" Brenda said.

"Sit around and look weird like you always do," Latonya said.

They joined the dinner. Brenda did her part. Looking at the poor lobster laid out on her plate was more than she could abide.

"Oren Bell." Aunt Grace walked around the table and

gave him a nudge and a loud whisper. "I don't like to worry Sarah over her failure in raising up her children, but Brenda isn't touching her dinner. Lobsters cost money, you know."

"I know," he whispered back inside her big ear, so nobody could hear. "Me and Latonya don't want to bother Mama on this happy occasion either. Brenda has something serious to be weird about."

"What? I won't tell poor Sarah."

"Another ghost is trying to give Brenda his message."

"I don't believe in ghosts. Is that Spiro Spill back again?"

"No, it's not Spiro."

"Who?"

"Fred Lightfoot is trying to contact Brenda, Aunt Grace. Don't you let it get around."

"Oh, land, that boy was a bushel of trouble when he was alive, and it doesn't surprise me to hear he is still causing mental distress for the family. Oren, trust me. I won't breathe a word of it."

Oren noted that quite a few of the guests were showing an interest, but Mama and Jack were at the far end of the table and talking to each other. He took a bite of his lobster, and it tasted good. He watched Aunt Grace talking to Dora and Teddy.

The rehearsal at the church was a walk-through. Aunt Grace addressed the reverend. "Reverend, if that man, who is not the actual father of the bride, can't make it down the aisle for the rehearsal, I believe he should be disqualified."

The reverend was polite but didn't pay no mind to Aunt Grace. Oren figured if a minister didn't listen to Aunt Grace, they didn't have to worry that the mayor would act on her complaints.

Mr. Shell and Ms. Pugh were doing a guitar duet of "The Wedding Song." They sounded beautiful. Latonya had done a fine job. The wedding might come off. It just might.

On the way home Mama and Jack discussed money. Mama said she would settle for a trip to Niagara Falls. Jack said the tickets for the cruise were bought and paid for, so the lobster and steak would have to stay on his credit card. They would still be gone three days. This would be ample time for the Friends of Fred.

Chapter 11

○   ○   ○

"Oren, pay attention. Mama, Brenda, and I are leaving now to have our hair done. At twelve o'clock you accompany Granddaddy and Jack to the hotel and check them into the rooms reserved under Jack's name. See that the groom and the appointed father of the bride are suited up properly, after which you will get them to the church on time. Don't let me down."

"Jack and I are adults, Latonya," Granddaddy said. "We don't need Oren Bell to tell us how to put on our pants."

"I don't want to get my hair done," Brenda said.

"This is not the day for me to listen to your wants or not wants, young lady," Latonya said.

Latonya took him aside before she joined Mama and Brenda in the van. "Oren, it's the best man's responsibility to take total care of the groom. It's my fear and suspicion that Jack might be a fainter."

"You don't have to worry. Jack operates on sick animals. He gets his hands in guts every day. He wants to get married to Mama bad. He was strong and joyful at

111

the rehearsal. He's a clock watcher when it comes to being on time. The man loves to get dressed up in good clothes. What makes you fear he's a fainter?"

"Just a feeling. Jack wants a family so bad, it makes him breathless."

Mama gave a honk on the horn, and Latonya had to leave him on that. He gave what she'd said a quick think. Jack wasn't perfect, but he was rock solid.

Granddaddy and Skid had gone back to sleep. Oren and Tuffcity went outside on the porch and smelled the fresh morning air. There was nobody on the Fred Field, but it looked like it was going to be a beautiful day for summer games. He decided to take a hike over to Canfield Street. Along the way he started to train Tuffcity to heel beside him without being leashed.

At first sight the art project looked deserted. He found both Mr. Sandman and the Goon Eye painting on canvas inside the shed.

"It's warm and dry today. How come you're inside?" he said.

"One of Mr. Sandman's pictures was wrecked outside, so we feel like working inside today," the Goon Eye said.

"Which picture?" Oren asked.

"The house with the red windows." Mr. Sandman said sadly. "It was on an easel outside the shed, and someone slashed it with a knife. I often leave my work outside for others to enjoy. Nobody has damaged any part of the project before."

The damaged picture faced the wall. Mr. Sandman turned it around for Oren. The red windows in the picture had been slashed out. The accusing and melancholy expression on the face of the house had been replaced by one of shock and horror. Was Brenda's arrangement of toys by the tree responsible? He tried to catch the Goon Eye's attention with a wink and a lift of his eyebrow, but he was busy creating a picture of his own.

"What's the theme?" Oren asked.

The Goon Eye was using bright primary colors and going at it like he had a purpose, but what the picture was going to be was not obvious.

"I'm carrying out the theme that Mr. Sandman saw in our artwork by the tree. Molested children is my concern. My picture portrays children who are being hurt all over the world—today, a hundred years ago, and tomorrow. My picture's timeless, you might say. Anyway Mr. Sandman says."

"I can see the children, but those big balls are out of their reach," Oren said.

"Those aren't balls, Oren. Those are circles of joy. If the children find them, they can jump inside and be safe."

Oren could see that the picture was going to make a statement. The Goon Eye was taking to art the way Fred had taken to music. He sure hoped that Skyler Sims found a circle of joy and didn't end up like Fred Lightfoot.

"Are you coming to the wedding?" Oren asked.

"Mr. and Mrs. Sandman said I could go with them," the Goon Eye said with some pride. "I want to be there, but Dora asked me to sit with the children so Teddy can be her escort to the wedding. She's thinking about taking me back full-time."

Maybe having Teddy at the wedding would give the Friends a chance to do a little haunting. He decided to check out the project.

"Dora sent Teddy to the store," the Goon Eye said. "But keep an eye out."

Tuffcity sniffed along beside him. The slate had been taken away from the doll's arms, but the rest was undisturbed. The broken cookie jar still said FRED. Maybe the killer hadn't seen it. Oren said good-bye to the two artists and walked on home with his pup at his heels.

It was sure a nice day. "Happy is the bride that the sun shines on." Latonya had sung those words when she saw the weather report on television.

"Please, Lord"—Oren offered up a quick prayer—"let Mama be happy in all kinds of weather forever and ever. Amen."

The groom was sitting on the front porch. Jack did not look totally well. Oren sat down beside him.

"How's it going, Jack? You ready for the Big Day or what?"

"The moment that I hoped and prayed for is at hand. I wish Latonya wasn't making a major production out of it."

"Latonya does make major productions out of things," Oren admitted.

"I never had a family before, Oren. Have I told you how I grew up in the Methodist Children's Home?"

Many times, but it would be a good a time to listen to it again.

"I always studied hard to gain the approval of teachers and adults. I stayed out of trouble. I was a good-looking kid. I don't know why I was never adopted. My real mother signed away her rights to me on the day I was born. I put myself through college and grad school working full-time jobs and part-time jobs. I was always serious and hardworking. I don't know why nobody ever wanted me."

"We want you, Jack. Just because a person's a nerd when he's a kid doesn't mean he can't improve."

"I'm trying to improve."

" 'Serious and hardworking' isn't all bad. I think Mama liked that in you right from the start. The family already has Latonya for 'positive' and Granddaddy for 'cool.' I'm what Mama calls 'solid'—but life isn't always positive, cool, or solid, so we have Brenda. You see, Jack, our family can use 'serious and hardworking.' You don't need to change or improve. We pretty much like you the way you are."

"Thank you, Oren, my best man. What do I do now? You're in charge of the groom."

"We have to take our wedding duds and Granddaddy to the hotel so the women can have the house to get ready. You stay here and don't think. I'm going to try to get Granddaddy moving."

"If I ever needed a drink, I need one now," Granddaddy said. "I walked steadier when I was drinking, Oren."

"You take a drink of anything but pure Detroit city water, and Latonya will break both our heads. C'mon, Granddaddy, we need to check into the hotel. You'll have time to take a nap and eat."

"One drink wouldn't hurt. One drink wouldn't be enough to make a preacher drunk."

"It's not my responsibility if the preacher turns up drunk."

Jack should have been helping him with Granddaddy, but Jack was all spaced out. Being a best man was no easy job. It would have been easier if he could have gotten them dressed at home, but Latonya said there was some kind of a rule about the groom not seeing the bride before the ceremony. Oren finally got both Jack, Granddaddy, and the white suits loaded into the car. Being behind the wheel of his Mustang focused Jack a little bit.

"I always dreamed of driving a Mustang when I was an orphan in the Methodist Children's Home."

"Now you got one to drive, Jack. Enjoy."

"And I'm about to have a family, a beautiful wife, and three wonderful children, and a father. God, I'm happy."

Jack was breathing funny and had the hiccups. Oren spied Granddaddy's hand digging down deep into a pocket. He brought up a package of mints. So far, so good, though Granddaddy could have slipped out and secured some booze while the best man had been off at Canfield Street.

The hotel was shaped like a tall roll of toilet paper. High on the top floor he could see across the river to

Windsor, Ontario, and in the other direction as far as Ohio. Oren had never stayed in a hotel with room service before. This hotel room was too fine for an afternoon of changing clothes. This room was the best. Oren suspected that Mama and Jack were going to come back and rest up here before their honeymoon trip.

By three o'clock it was time for him to move the two of them out to the church. Jack was dressed and fooling around with his tie. Oren had let Granddaddy sleep until the last minute because that seemed safer. It turned out Granddaddy was wrong. He wasn't capable of getting his pants on by himself.

Oren tried to hurry them. "Blue's brother is waiting downstairs to drive us to the church. A cop will know how to cut through the Fourth of July traffic coming in from the 'burbs.''

"How's it going to look to arrive at the church with a cop?" Granddaddy said. "The guests will think Jack got off a few hours from prison to marry Sarah. That often happens.''

"Officer Brown won't be wearing his uniform, and he's driving his own car. Move it.''

Jack and Granddaddy didn't look that well put together, but they moved. All three of them had ties that were untied because Jack didn't remember how to do it. Oren sure didn't know how. Mama could help them, but they were not allowed to see her before the wedding. When they arrived at the church, the reverend took Oren and Jack to a little room next to the altar. Granddaddy was led off to be with Mama and the bridesmaids.

Fine and cool. Granddaddy was now Latonya's responsibility, and Oren could put his total concentration on
Jack. Jack still had the hiccups, and his shallow breathing was making his face blotchy. When the other
groomsman arrived, the reverend said it was time for
him and Oren to go out and seat the guests. The new
man's name was Luke and he knew how to tie their ties.
Luke was supposed to seat Jack's friends and family on
one side of the aisle, and Oren was supposed to seat
Mama's friends on the other.

"Jack, I have to leave you. Will you be okay?"

"Do you have to go, Oren?" Jack said.

"I'll be back."

Mama had more people coming on her side, so
they decided to mix it up. Oren offered his arm to
Mrs. Sandman. Mr. Sandman followed them down the
aisle.

"You look very handsome, Oren," Mrs. Sandman said.

He stood taller. "Thank you, ma'am. Sorry Skyler
couldn't attend the wedding with you and Mr.
Sandman."

"We were hoping he would, but this afternoon Skyler
asked Dora to take him back as a foster child. She
agreed to accept him and to call Social Services but
Marcus believes the boy has potential as an artist, and if
he stays with Dora, she'll never let him work with us."

When Dora Dillworthy and Teddy came in, Oren offered Dora his arm and escorted her to their seats. He
was chilled and conscious of the killer walking behind.
Aunt Grace came in with Dink and Dede. She was still

miffed because her children didn't have a bigger role in the wedding. Latonya had proposed to let Dink help seat the guests and put the runners down, but Aunt Grace had said that wasn't good enough. She had also declined to give a reading from the Bible. She suggested the marriage would suffer with no Bible reading, but it would not be her fault.

"Would you like to sit in the front or in the back, Aunt Grace?" Oren asked.

"In the middle on an end seat, if you please," Aunt Grace said.

Blue and Whitey came in with their families.

"Looking fine, bro," Blue said.

Blue's mother and Whitey's aunt told him how handsome he looked. Oren was going to give them prime seats down front, but he had an excellent idea. He put them smack in front of Dora and Teddy.

"Blue and Whitey, could you come to the back of the church? I need you to put the runners down on the floor before the bridesmaids step down the aisle. I'll show you how. You'll have time to go back and take your seats before the ceremony begins."

"Listen, you guys," he said when they were a careful distance from the guests. "I can only tell you this once. There's a trumpet player up in the balcony who's going to play with the organist when the Wedding March begins. I'm seating you directly in front of Teddy and Dora. The trumpet will blow one measure before the organ joins in and the first bridesmaid comes down the aisle. Blue, you say to Whitey so that nobody can hear except

Teddy, 'That sounds like Fred playing the trumpet.' Be in the right place at the right time and do it subtle. You can't disturb the people marching down the aisle or the people watching. Nobody but Teddy has to hear it. Can you manage that?"

"It won't be Fred playing the trumpet, will it?" Whitey said.

"Don't worry, Oren," Blue said. "I got the message."

When Wesley and her folks came in, Oren seated them behind Dora and Teddy. He didn't have time to talk to Wesley, but she knew she was supposed to back up any Fred-ghost action. He hoped that the Friends of Fred would keep this covert action slick and low so it wouldn't interrupt any vows.

It was nearly time. Oren and Luke returned to the little room where the reverend and Jack were waiting. Luke told Jack that the church was filled with guests. When Jack went to answer back, his voice was gone, but he was still hiccupping.

"Jack, can you say 'I do'? Say it for me," Oren said.

Jack opened his mouth, and nothing came out but a *hic*. The beautiful strains of Ms. Pugh and Mr. Shell strumming on their guitars and singing "The Wedding Song" came through the door. The reverend opened the door so they could listen better. Tears were coming out of Jack's eyes. When Ms. Pugh and Mr. Shell were done, Blue and Whitey put the runner down. Oren saw them seat themselves with dignity. There was a second of silent waiting. From somewhere up on the balcony came the beautiful, somber wail of a trumpet, the first-chair trumpeter from Northwestern High School Band. The organ joined the trumpet, and together they played music fit for the processional of a queen. Mr. Shell had told Oren and Latonya that this march was "Trumpet Voluntary." It was awesome. Oren decided to practice so someday he could play that good at somebody's wedding. It was time for the groom and groomsmen to march out of their little room.

"Jack, walk straight, hold your head high, and speak up when it's your time. You do that and I'll be a Daniels for you when it's over."

Oren said this softly. Maybe later he could deny that he had said it. The reverend led them out in a straight and serious line. Jack sure looked like he was going to the electric chair.

Brenda came down first. She had on a long yellow dress and she was carrying a basket of fresh-picked flowers. She kept step to the music and did not look too weird. So far, so good. Mama's friend came down the aisle and stood beside Luke. Latonya was next. He had been looking at his twin sister for a lifetime but not seeing her as being a real person. Latonya had looked like a grown woman for a time now, but today in her yellow dress she looked different. She looked like a pretty girl. Latonya stood next to him. Half a year ago Latonya had been taller than him. Now she had on heels, and they stood together even.

The volume of the trumpet and organ turned so high, it filled up his senses and overflowed down to his toes. All of the guests must have felt the same way, because they stood up. Mama was coming down the aisle on Granddaddy's arm. One time Brenda had asked Oren if beautiful angels were ever black. The way Mama looked answered Brenda's question. She wore a long white dress with a halo of white flowers around her head. Oren was afraid that the sight of such beauty would be too much for Jack. He poked him.

Jack said, "I do."

"Not yet, Jack."

Granddaddy was walking tall. He held a cane on the arm that wasn't holding Mama, but he didn't seem to need it. Oren was sighing in relief, when he saw something terrible about to happen. Aunt Grace stuck her big foot out in front of Granddaddy. Without looking at Aunt Grace or her foot, Granddaddy slammed down on her foot with his cane and kept on marching. Aunt Grace avoided screaming in pain, but it must have hurt. None of the guests were in a position to see what almost happened, and Oren was grateful. The Lord was on duty and on their side.

Jack took Mama for his wife loud and clear. His hiccups were gone like magic, but his face was still wet. When Mama and Jack kissed, Oren knew they were married. The trumpet and organ started to play the recessional. Oren offered Latonya his arm. She took it and smiled at him. Latonya had arranged a perfect wedding, and he and the Friends of Fred were going to put Tedfield Jones behind bars forever.

While the rest of the wedding party were still hugging and shaking hands on the receiving line, Oren and

Latonya joined Wesley, Blue, and Whitey at the side of the church. Mama, Jack, Granddaddy, and Brenda were going back to the hotel to rest up for the reception. Oren, Latonya, and Wesley had to go with Mr. Shell to join the band.

"How did it go?" he said.

"Perfect," Wesley answered. "Blue leaned across and nearly on top of Tedfield Jones. He whispered at me, 'Nobody plays that C note like Fred. It's him. He's back.' Then he said to Teddy and Dora. 'Sorry, ma'am. Sorry, sir.' I thought Blue being polite was a nice touch. My mom and dad told me to sit back and keep quiet, and Blue's mother did the same to him. Whitey kept saying 'I know that C note. It was Fred,' until his aunt threatened to take him home."

"It was Fred," Whitey said.

"That was real wicked. I love it," Latonya said.

"Did anyone else hear you?" Oren asked Wesley.

"We were discreet, but some might have heard. Did you notice Teddy's face when he came through the reception line?"

"He looked disturbed enough, but you know what worries me?" Oren said. "The Goon Eye put himself back inside Dora's household. He's bent on caring for the younger children. He could be in great danger."

"We have to speed this up," Latonya said.

Mr. Shell came out of the church with his two instrument cases in hand and herded them to Mama's van. Aunt Grace came limping up with Dink and Dede. Oren piled in first. The first-chair trumpeter was sitting in the backseat.

"You did a nice job," Oren said.

"Thank you, man."

Chapter 12

○   ○   ○

"The Fourth of July is my favorite holiday of the whole year," Dink said.

"Why?" Most of Dink's remarks did not require listening to or answering, but Oren was mildly interested in why a whipped kid like Dink would favor one holiday over another. Wesley butted in. Women were like that. They never gave a fellow a chance to ponder.

"My favorite holiday is Halloween. Last Halloween I dressed up like an endangered species."

Oren interrupted Wesley's boring story. "Why do you favor the Fourth of July, Dink Dooley?"

"Because I'm sitting outside on a beautiful night in a bandstand with my friends and a famous high school band, and best of all, my mother is nowhere around."

"That is rather unusual," Latonya said. "Where is Aunt Grace?"

"Decorating the Detroit Boat Club for the reception," Dink said proudly. "She went on ahead so as she could surprise Aunt Sarah and Uncle Jack."

Oren wondered how Aunt Grace could screw up the reception.

"That's a wonderful thing for your mother to do," Latonya said.

"We're having a fine time together, aren't we, brothers and sisters?" Dink maintained. "Let's do it again next Fourth of July."

"Where's Mr. Shell?" Latonya said. "The senior high band people are getting restless."

The band members were teenagers. If there was no old person around to curb them, it didn't take them long to lapse into riot. The wind and percussion sections were all talking and shouting to each other. Latonya's brain had a screen to separate the bad words from the good, but poor Wesley's pale face was turning from pink to pinker. A mama's boy like Dink shouldn't have to listen to such stuff. There were lots of holiday people starting to gather to see what the band was about. Where was Mr. Shell? He should be taking command. Ms. Pugh arrived and positioned herself in front of the band. She had a microphone, but she was still having a time getting their attention.

"People," she shouted. "Mr. Shell has taken ill."

Latonya gasped, and Wesley moaned, but Ms. Pugh went on to explain that it was only a few chest pains. The emergency room in the hospital where she had taken him wanted to test them out.

"Who's going to direct us?" a trombone player shouted.

"I'm going to direct you," Ms. Pugh shouted back. "Take your places.

"What qualifications you got, little lady?" the bass drummer demanded.

"I know this music and I'm going to direct this band. Now, move, people. It's show time."

They took their places, but there was a mumble that could have turned into a rumble. The bass drummer gave Wesley a push that sent her sprawling. Ms. Pugh came flying up to Wesley's rescue. Actually Oren wanted to rescue Wesley, but Ms. Pugh got there first. Wesley's band uniform had protected her from cuts, but she was shaken up.

"Marilla Moore, why are you bothering Wesley?" Ms. Pugh demanded.

"We don't need no cymbals for *The 1812 Overture,* and the girl's white face don't belong here," Marilla said.

"What we don't need here is hate and shove," Ms. Pugh said. "Marilla, you get off the bandstand and go find a merry-go-round in the park to ride. *The 1812 Overture* requires grown-up musicians. Wesley is taking over on drums. Now, the rest of you band people listen good. I have been witness to many of your practices. I have the heart and will to direct you and I am going to do it."

Marilla skulked away like she was relieved to be off from a concert that was bound to bring humiliation on the famous Northwestern High School Band. Ms. Pugh went down and stood in front of them, and she looked taller than before. She tapped the stand a few times. She said they would do a warm-up number that they were familiar with to bring in the crowd. They all knew "The Washington Post March." Ms. Pugh waved her arms. It was music they had performed many times before, so it came off medium well done. A crowd had gathered by the time they had finished. Oren saw Blue and Whitey. Ms. Pugh bowed her head like she was praying. They were all very quiet and watched her intently. She raised her arms and brought them down. *The 1812 Overture* took off, not too fast, not too slow, the excitement building the way it should. When they finally came to the grand finish, the cannons went off. The crowd clapped and clapped because they really liked those cannons. They couldn't stop.

It sure felt good to come to the end of a successful concert and take the bows for it. They ran to the comfort station to change their clothes. Now they could hike across the island and enjoy their wedding reception.

When they first entered the room, Dink said. "Look, my mother had Aunt Sarah's red windows put up on the wall. She knew they would be the perfect decoration. They sure look right, don't they?"

The Detroit Boat Club was old and grand, and the beautiful windows were postioned high over the table where the bridal party was seated. The windows were watching the guests.

"I wonder how she managed," Oren said.

"I gave her the keys to our house," Latonya admitted. "I don't know how she got them so high on the wall. She must have come over before the wedding. They look secure enough."

Oren took his place at the head table between Jack and Granddaddy. The guests kept banging their spoons against the table, this being some kind of signal for Jack to kiss Mama. Oren turned to Granddaddy.

"Granddaddy, did Aunt Grace mean to do us a favor by displaying the red eyes of the house?"

"Good and bad intentions are all the same for Grace."

That about summed it up. "Do you know anything about Mr. Shell?"

"Pugh's gone to the hospital to stay with him. Teaching music to children is no job for a Music Man to do. I knew sooner or later the stress of such work would weaken Carl's heart." Granddaddy shook his head sadly like Mr. Shell was a goner.

Oren studied the tables of guests. Aunt Grace and her children had themselves seated at the table with the reverend. Dora and Tedfield were at the same table as Wesley and her folks. He wondered how the seating arrangement could be used to the purpose of the Friends of Fred. Poor old Goon Eye was missing all the fun.

"Oren," Latonya whispered in his ear. "Brenda should be sitting at the bride-and-groom table. The church ladies are setting up the food. Go find her."

He peeked into the other rooms of the Detroit Boat Club. He went outside. Had she fallen into the river? He went back inside and motioned to Wesley to come and help him find her.

"I can't find Brenda anywhere."

"That's because she's underneath our table."

"What's she doing there?"

"She's telling Teddy that the eyes are watching him. She's repeating it over and over, and Teddy is too scared to look under the table. Dora is talking to my folks, and nobody hears her little voice except Teddy and me. Don't worry, Oren. She's keeping it low-key."

"She needs to get back to our table because it's time to fall in the food line, and the bridal party goes first."

"She can't come out until it's time for our table to go get their food."

That Brenda was really something. What if Teddy did look under the table? Sooner or later even a psyched-out killer would do that if he heard little voices. Teddy couldn't kill Brenda in the middle of a wedding reception. Could he? When Oren returned, he told Mama and Latonya, "Brenda's in the ladies' room. She says for us to go ahead and get our food. She'll be back as soon as she's washed up."

When Oren saw Teddy and Dora in the food line, Brenda slipped in and joined them.

"You stay here by me, Miss," Latonya said. "And make sure you take some vegetables."

It was Oren's duty as best man to give the toast. He stood up, and every guest gave him their attention. He had thought about what to say, and practiced. Latonya had given him some advice.

"My sisters, Latonya and Brenda, my grandfather, Bill Bell, and me, want to thank all of you for coming here to celebrate the marriage of our mother and Jack. Jack, as you all know, is a veterinarian. Our family met him when he made a house call to treat our pets. Jack saved the lives of our pup and cat. When Jack saw Sarah, it was love at first sight for him, and it didn't take our mother long to return his love. It might have been second or third sight for me and my sisters, but now we love Jack and we are a family until death do us part. Special thanks to the Fry family and the Brown family for all their help in making this celebration a success. Mr. Carl Shell and Ms. Pat Pugh did a bang-up job on the music, but Mr. Shell took ill and can't be with us. We hope and pray he will be back with us soon. And now I would like to give thanks to our aunt Grace. She has always been right there with her advice, but what she did tonight was special. Those beautiful red-glass windows on the wall are something to see, and Aunt Grace thought to put them there. Those windows were Jack's engagement gift to our mother. For more years than any of us here were alive, they looked down on our neighborhood from the deserted house next door. They saw everything good and evil that went on in the neighborhood. Those windows were our late, great friend Fred Lightfoot's eyes to the world. Aunt Grace knows how much our family misses Fred. Thank you, Aunt Grace, for knowing all this and bringing the windows today."

Latonya nudged him. He told them again what a great guy Jack was, thanked them all for coming, and sat down. He could feel Latonya thinking he had said too much. Jack and Mama both leaned over and told him that he had made a fine toast. He noted with relief that Granddaddy was toasting with water and not champagne. Aunt Grace got up from her table and came over and hugged him.

"Thank you, Oren, for appreciating what I did. Most people never do."

When Aunt Grace sat down again and all the guests were busy eating, Latonya said, "When I told you to give some thanks to Aunt Grace for her effort, what you said wasn't what I had in mind, but it worked. You know, Oren, all of us but Mama are guilty of finding fault with Aunt Grace but never giving her credit. You may have broken ground here."

Before he could get any food to his mouth, Granddaddy came over to take his ear.

"Oren, you see that lady sitting over at the far table? The one in the long blue dress?"

"I see the one you mean."

"Well, that is your true grandmother, Betty Bell. She may call herself by a different name nowadays, but make no mistake, that's her."

Oren took a careful look. Granddaddy had been married many times, and they hadn't all been church weddings. He had always claimed that Betty Bell was their true grandmother, but Aunt Grace said there was no proof of that.

"Granddaddy, you always said Betty Bell was mean and ugly. That's one handsome lady."

"You notice that she has on a long dress? The truth is, poor Betty is a bit bowlegged and she had a bad temper. It appears to me that she has improved with age. When the music starts up, I think I'll ask her to dance."

"Should you put your legs to such a test?"

"I'm bracing my trembling limbs for the effort. I think I can manage a slow dance."

Mama and Jack had to dance the first dance before anybody else could take to the floor. It was about time for the fireworks to begin. Oren and Latonya went off to find Wesley. Brenda was missing. Was she off haunting Teddy?

"Oren, Latonya, guess what?" Wesley said. "I told my father how the Goon Eye was missing everything. My father asked Teddy and Dora if he could bring the Goon Eye and the children to the fireworks. The Friends of Fred will all be here."

"But not all who cared for him. Ms. Pugh has gone to the hospital to stay with Mr. Shell," Oren said. "Wesley, what was Teddy's response to my toast? Did you notice?"

"He stared at the windows over your head while you were talking. He told Dora he was leaving, but she wouldn't let him."

The fireworks couldn't start until the sky was dark, and the summer daylight held on for a time. The crowd was moving outside.

"How did you like our cannons at the close of your concert?" Blue said.

"That wasn't you and Whitey doing the cannons," Oren said.

"We were the ones to tell them when," Blue said. "Mr. Shell assigned us to do that before he had his heart trouble. I hope Mr. Shell lives to give us credit for it.

C'mon, Oren. It's time for the first fireworks to go off. Let's go."

Latonya and Wesley needed to find Brenda.

"You guys go ahead, Blue."

This time Brenda really was in the ladies' room. Latonya went in and brought her out.

"I had to wash the sugar off my hands," Brenda explained. "While old Teddy was on the dance floor with Dora, I made his sugar cubes spell FRED."

"I've said it before and I'll say it again," Latonya said. "Brenda Bell is a genius, but you back off from haunting Tedfield Jones, girl. You hear? He's a dangerous man, and you are a child."

The reception room was nearly empty when Mr. Fry walked in with the Goon Eye, a little girl of about eight years, and two boys who looked to be about four. They were clinging to the Goon Eye.

"There's a balcony upstairs where we can get a terrific view," Oren said.

"That's excellent, man. Cammie, George, and Jojo are afraid of crowds."

There wasn't a chance to talk, because the first firecracker was blasting a steady path to its bright, short life in the sky. It was the first time any of them had seen such high-quality fireworks. Oren stayed cool, but it was an impressive sight. The explosives were being set off by men on barges in the river. As the firecracker exploded, you saw the people across the river in Canada. When the dying fireflies of color descended into the water, you could see the men on the boats scurrying around like little bugs. It was totally awesome. When it was finally over, Latonya and Wesley took Cammie, George, and Jojo downstairs to have some wedding food. The Goon Eye turned to Brenda.

"I don't know how you're doing it, but Teddy is spooked." He told Dora those red windows are after him, but she told him to stop talking crazy, or she'll get herself a new man. Fred always warned Teddy that the house would take care of anybody who hurt him. What do we do next?"

"I don't know," Oren said. "But, Brenda, you got to quit your haunting. Let us older kids bring Teddy down."

"You aren't doing it fast enough," Brenda said.

"Goon Eye, how is Teddy around Dora's children?" Oren changed the subject.

"He hasn't been bothering them. He touches one of them wrong and I kill him," the Goon Eye said.

Most of the guests were gone. Granddaddy had disappeared with Betty Bell. Jack and Mr. Sandman freed the windows and lifted them gently off the wall.

"Let the honeymoon begin," Latonya sang out.

"If you don't have enough money for your cruising, Sarah and Jack, I discovered that I have a little put aside in my cookie jar," Aunt Grace said.

"I can pay for my own honeymoon, thank you," Jack said.

"You save what you have for a rainy day, Grace. Jack and I will manage, but thank you for your generous offer." Mama drew Oren aside. "Oren, Latonya and Brenda are staying the night with Wesley. The Sandmans have offered to take the girls to Grosse Pointe. I have no idea where your grandfather has taken himself off to. Jack and I will bring you and the windows back to our house. You lock yourself in."

"No problem, Mama."

"I'd feel better if Granddaddy and Latonya were with you."

"Don't worry, Mama."

Mama must really trust him. He and Jack wrapped the windows in a borrowed tablecloth, and Oren held them in his lap all the way home.

Mama and Jack hugged him good-bye. "Here's the telephone number of the hotel," Jack said.

The doors were all locked, and Oren was alone in the house with the pup, Skid, and the windows.

Chapter 13

○   ○   ○

I t was two hours past midnight. He decided to take the pup and cat into the purple bedroom where the girls usually slept. This was the room where Brenda's ghost, Spiro Spill, used to hang out. Where were the real ghosts when you needed them? Skid didn't follow him, but Tuffcity climbed up on the bed and went right to sleep. Oren couldn't sleep without his old cat. On bare feet he padded back to the living room.

"C'mon, Skid. It's no lumpy sofa for us tonight."

Skid looked up at him, but refused to move. A moonbeam or a headlight coming from outside made the cat's eyes shine in the dark. Skid's eyes were yellow, but they had the same glaring, staring quality as the red glass. It might be easier to move Tuffcity into the living room. Oren padded back to the bedroom.

"C'mon, Tuffcity. We got to stick together. We're going to sleep in the living room with Skid."

Tuffcity thumped his tail once, but he didn't even take his head off the pillow. He was timid, but when a police car or a fire engine went by, he howled like a hound from hell. Oren pulled on his collar.

"It's your duty to follow your master."

The pup went limp. Oren was going to sleep with either a stubborn cat or a chicken dog.

He arranged his body around the lumps on the sofa. Skid circled and settled on his chest. Oren moved a little to get a spring out of his back, and Skid growled at him to lie still. The clock struck three. When it struck the half hour, Oren was still awake. The ticking of the clock was too loud tonight. His brain was on full alert. He heard something outside the house. The wind was stirring the grass and gusting the papers around the yard. Did he hear footsteps in the grass? He listened. The third step coming up to the porch always creaked when anyone stepped on it. Someone with cautious feet was coming up onto the porch. Granddaddy walked heavy with a cane. Nothing more for fifty-five ticks and then a key being put into the lock. The key was hard to catch and turn. Someone who wasn't familiar with the lock was taking the key out and trying again.

Twitches like little heartbeats were popping up all over his body. Skid got off his chest and left. Oren picked the sofa cover up from the floor and covered himself as the door swung slowly open. He uncovered his eyes. The intruder stood in the middle of the room like he wasn't sure which way to turn or where to go. Oren didn't move or breathe. The slightest sound would betray him. The headlights from a passing car on Fourth Street flashed across the room, and Oren saw the face of the killer.

Tedfield Jones crossed to the dining room. He didn't

see Oren. He hadn't seen the Goon Eye in the shadows of Fred's room.

Tedfield stood still as a statue in the middle of the room. The prickles on Oren's back and arms demanded that he move. He took a few steady breaths. The springs in the sofa groaned, but the statue didn't move. Teddy appeared to be facing the buffet.

Oren's position was dangerous, but he had the advantage of surprise, and something else: an electric wire sizzling in his gut. All he could think was:

> Dear Lord,
> Grant me the strength
> to bring Fred's killer down.

Still wrapped in the sofa scarf, he rolled. The springs groaned, and he hit the floor with a thump. Oren lay still on the floor, expecting to be kicked or shot. He counted a hundred ticks. Nothing. He crawled behind Granddaddy's chair. A hundred more ticks. He crawled into the dining room.

The city lights illuminated the eerie scene. Teddy turned around. His mad eyes darted around the room, but he didn't see Oren. He was hypnotized by Skid crouched between the two panels of red glass. Oren could see the cat's dark form because he knew it was there, but the glaring yellow eyes staring fixedly between the two red ones were all that Teddy saw.

"I'll shoot out all four of your damned eyes."

A distant siren passed, followed by a low howl from

Tuffcity in the bedroom. An answering screech came from the eyes on the buffet. Oren gave an ear-splitting yell and lunged out and grabbed Teddy around the ankles. Skid leaped forward onto Teddy's head.

The gun had dropped from his hand. His face was in the rug.

"Let me alone, Fred. I didn't mean to do it. You made me do it."

Skid scratched Teddy's face bad and then took off. Teddy tried to heave up, but Oren pinned him with a terrible power. "No!" he howled like an animal. He dug his fingers into Teddy's back. There came a loud *thump, thump, thump*. His heart or Teddy's heart? No, it was outside. Granddaddy. Oren hoped Betty Bell was with him, because by all accounts she was one scary lady. The sound of the cane made Teddy moan. Oren held fast. The key turned. The lamp went on, and Dora Dillworthy charged in behind Granddaddy.

"Tedfield Jones," Dora screamed. "Grace told me you took her key. You trying to steal from these folks?"

"Get Fred off my back."

"Fred?"

"Fred Lightfoot. Get his ghost off my back."

"That's Oren Bell on your back, you idiot. What did you do to Fred?"

Dora charged Ted, but Granddaddy pulled her back. Oren released the trembling man and let Granddaddy pin him with his cane.

"Oren, you did your duty. I'll take over. Dora, your man has more than breaking and entering on his head. If

Teddy killed the most promising little trumpeter of this century, we'll help you put him away for the rest of his miserable life. Call the cops, Oren, before I sic all the ghosts in hell on this blubbering fool."

While they waited for the police, Teddy pleaded with Dora. His face was covered with blood. He looked pitiful.

"I didn't do nothin' to Fred, Dora. Honest. I always liked the boy. I just wanted to shoot out them cursed windows. Them windows are the red eyes of the devil and they're out to get me."

"Such foolish talk," Dora said, softening a bit. "You are too taken with ghosts, my man."

He'll beat it again, Oren thought. He felt cold. *Ted will plead crazy and say he didn't kill Fred.*

Granddaddy was guarding Ted. Oren slipped inside the purple bedroom and took his old Spiro Spill trumpet from underneath the bed. Tuffcity looked on with concern. Oren held the instrument in his hand and looked to the ceiling.

"I think it does have to be you playing it this time, Fred, 'cause the sound has to drive Teddy over."

Granddaddy had shown Fred a special way to play Taps. He said there was no use him showing Oren or Dink how to do it. They didn't have the lip or the talent. Oren inserted the mouthpiece and put the trumpet to his lips. The notes lifted through the early-morning air, each one perfect until he reached the highest, then he cracked that one note on purpose to denote sadness and then came back down each note perfect. Oren put the horn down and rubbed his wet face in Tuffcity's fur. A warm tongue washed away his tears.

When the police arrived, Tedfield Jones confessed to killing Fred Lightfoot. Granddaddy stared down at his toes. Dora looked like she was about to explode. Teddy pleaded for police protection from the spirits that hounded him and from the wrath of Dora Dillworthy. The police took Dora to the station because they wanted to question her along with Teddy.

Oren and Granddaddy sat at the dining room table as the first light came through the red panes. The morning sun showed that the bloody eyes were just windows. They could reflect only what good or bad people chose to see through them.

"Granddaddy, did you know that Teddy was Fred's killer?"

"A few days ago I woke up one morning knowing that Teddy was the killer. It must have come to me in a dream. The impression put me in a rage, but I had no proof. Oren?"

"What?"

"If I was not a sober man, I'd swear I heard Fred blowing Taps in the purple bedroom. His special Taps to put troubled souls to rest."

They looked at each other. Finally Oren said, "About that dream, Granddaddy. Did the Goon Eye tell you who did it?"

"I think so. Maybe me hearing Fred blow Taps was a dream. Let's try to get a few hours' sleep to clear our minds of ghosts. I need a mug of chocolate, but neither of us is capable of heating it up right."

"I'm making some for Skid and Tuffcity. They deserve it." Oren stood up slowly. "How did your date with Betty Bell go?"

"If Betty thinks up some nice place to take me and rings me on the phone, I just might see her again, but I will rest up for the rest of the summer before I seriously consider it."

"Oren," Latonya said. "What did you say to Mama when she called?"

"I said, 'Everything is under control. Have a happy honeymoon.' "

It was later on, the same morning. The Friends of Fred were sitting around the dining room table. The windows glowed an innocent golden red. The story got better every time he told it, and it had been pretty good the way it happened.

"I don't approve of deceiving Mama, but she does deserve a happy honeymoon. Skyler, what did Dora say when she got home?"

"She asked me if it was true that Teddy beat on her children. She's had them to the hospital for pipe marks on their legs, but the woman never wanted to see. I told her everything I knew about Teddy and how he killed Fred. She believed me like she never would have before. She's going to take me to the station to tell my story. Dora said she would testify against the man in court. Latonya, can my children jump on your sofa?"

"Let them have their fun. We're getting a new one one of these days."

"How do we know that Fred really wasn't here last night?" Whitey said. "You tell me, Brenda."

"Well"—Brenda gave her expert opinion—"maybe he was. Ghosts are funny. Sometimes they don't make their presence known in the usual way. Fred was always the free spirit. He wouldn't want to lodge like a lump under the bed like poor old Spiro. I had these little tickles of inspiration inside my head when I was thinking of ways to spook Teddy. Teddy could have missed seeing the broken doll and the slate under the tree, but he did look and he did see. Teddy could have looked under the table and seen me when I was whispering my message, but he didn't look and he didn't see. He could have seen Skid lodged between the windows, but all he saw was the cat's eyes."

"The caper in the church worked perfect," Blue said. "When Wesley and me suggested the trumpeter in the balcony was Fred, Teddy took it as gospel truth."

"Fred was always a trickster and a magician. I think Fred was with us all along," Whitey said.

"Oren was given extra courage last night," Latonya said. "And the pup and cat had their timing right. It was some help that Tedfield Jones was a cowardly, drugged-up, and stupid man, but it does appear that Fred was the force in bringing the man to justice. What do you think, Oren?"

"When I played Taps in the purple bedroom early this

morning, I sounded too good to be me, but of course it was me."

"It takes giants to do battle with nightmares," Brenda said. "The Friends of Fred were the giants on the wall."

Latonya turned to Wesley. "Will you give us your report?"

"I called the hospital, and they said Mr. Shell has been released. I called Ms. Pugh and found out he was safe and sound at her place. It turns out that Mr. Shell had heartburn from all the lobster he ate at the rehearsal dinner. He's fine now."

"Thank you, Wesley," Latonya said. "Now Skyler has some news."

"When the police brought Dora home, the Sandmans went over to see what the fuss was all about. When Dora told them, Susan offered to take me and the children for a while. Dora said she appreciated the offer because she needed time to get her act together. I don't know if the Sandmans are going to be allowed to keep us, but for now Cammie, George, Jojo, and me are happy with the Sandmans. Mrs. Sandman will teach me how to read, and Mr. Sandman will encourage me in art. How about that?"

"Well, that's fine," Latonya said. "I guess now we'll have a free and peaceful ride through the rest of summer."

Chapter 14

o   o   o

A series of what Latonya called little miracles occurred in July. The first one was inspired by Mr. Shell.

"I would appreciate it, Bill, if you would start the beginning music students in some of the elementary procedures," Mr. Shell said to Granddaddy.

"I don't like beginners, Carl. They got too much to learn. I don't like advanced students either. They think they know too much."

"Well, I have a few from a middle school in East Detroit who are not beginning and are not advanced but show promise and are willing to learn."

"They sound about right. Send them over, and I'll try them out."

Granddaddy had been helping Oren and Latonya with their cornet and French horn, but he preferred teaching the boy and girl Mr. Shell sent over. They'd never heard any of his stories about how he'd once been a famous trumpeter. The best part was that the mothers paid Granddaddy by the hour.

Aunt Grace predicted that the money would eventually go for booze, because once a boozer, always a boozer. The thing about Aunt Grace's horrible predictions was you had to give them a little thought. Still, by mid-July, the Fourth and Hancock Music Studio was prospering. The house was filled with noise from Mr. Shell's upstairs students and Granddaddy's downstairs students.

Oren, Latonya, Wesley, Blue, and Whitey spent a few hours each day painting the outside of their Canfield Street house, while the Goon Eye whitewashed the inside. Each wall was to be a canvas for his or Brenda's pictures. Brenda would have a sunken or sinking ship room, as well as a deserted or demolished building room. The Goon Eye favored painting lost people. Brenda stressed melancholy, while the Goon Eye always gave his faces and figures a lifeline of hope. Mr. Sandman said both attitudes had their place in art.

Oren classified the Fred Field as his miracle. Each day ended with a tight game of baseball. The Pistols were mighty competition, but the Stooges held their own. Even Dink occasionally got a ball in from left field.

Another miracle was Mama's happiness. Before she left for work in the morning, she hugged and kissed Jack and then all the members of the family and the pets.

"Cut it out, Sarah," Granddaddy said. "I don't like it, and neither does Skid. All that hugging and kissing isn't a good example for the children. Another thing, Sarah, you're always singing and you can't carry a tune."

Before Jack, Mama had come home tired from her job. Now she had added hours of schoolwork to her regular job and she still came in the door full of energy. Jack was both a useful and an annoying addition. His stuff took up a lot of room. He was always telling Oren what he thought, and his opinions were dumb about most things, but it wasn't like Oren had to listen. Sometimes Mama made him. The girls were punch proud to have Jack for a father, and that was a little annoying.

"Latonya, do you think Jack is spoiling Brenda?"

"Everybody has always spoiled Brenda, but Jack is sure carrying through on it," Latonya admitted. "Still, when Brenda sasses Mama, Jack backs Mama up. He also backs Mama up when she puts limits on some of your unseemly activities, Oren Bell. And another thing, we have more money to pay the bills with Jack's paycheck. That's a blessing."

"He hasn't handed out much of that money to me or you, Latonya."

"Your wants are not needs, Oren. When you have a true need, Jack will provide."

In the fall they would take care of the adoption. July had thirty-one golden days, and each one was turning out better than the one before. The Bell-Daniels family had friends, neighbors, art, music, and baseball.

So much happiness. It wasn't natural.

Chapter 15

○　　○　　○

The third of August was a dog-hot day. Grand-daddy sat in front of a fan in his underwear. The pup and cat were laid out in a dopey sleep.

"It's a relief to know that Mama and Jack are working in air-conditioned offices," Latonya said.

"That sure is some relief," Whitey said.

"We could play ball," Oren said.

"We could go to the library," Latonya said.

"It's too hot to play ball or read," Blue said. "Let's watch TV. You Bells ought to get one of them remote-control things."

They watched the local news in a tranced-out state. There had been a triple murder on East Palmer, but it was nobody they knew.

"Hey," Blue said, "there's a man talking about our art project."

They all came to attention. A newscaster was standing in front of the Canfield Street Art Project. There were neighbors crowding around eager to get their faces on TV.

"The Canfield Project is an effort by local artists to

turn boarded-up houses into art objects," the man said. "Complaints have been coming to the mayor's office, causing a ripple. City officials say ripples cannot be ignored, and there is an order on the mayor's desk to demolish the project. Here's a gentleman passing by. Sir, do you live here on Canfield?"

"I live two streets over, but I walk by every day on my way to the bus stop. I don't like what I see. Looks like junk. My wife don't like it either."

"Marcus Sandman, the Detroit artist responsible for this work, has been recognized by art critics around the world," the interviewer said.

"My wife and I don't recognize him."

"Thank you, sir." The newscaster moved on to two ladies. One was Dora Dillworthy.

"I understand you ladies live right here on Canfield. What is your opinion?"

"What Marcus has done has a lot of love in it for his community, and I like it," the first lady said.

"It kind of grows on you," Dora said.

The newscaster turned to the camera. "One man's art is another man's junk, but it does appear that the Canfield Project is doomed."

Brenda was shaking all over. Latonya went over and took their little sister's hands in hers.

"Don't cry, Brenda. The mayor will never agree to hurt your project. Mr. Sandman took burned-out, rat-infested places and made something beautiful out of them."

"I don't believe you." Brenda sobbed. "You're a positive thinker. Oren, tell me true. Can the mayor knock down my art project?"

"Maybe Ms. Pugh would know. She knows about city officials and art," Oren hedged.

"I'm asking you."

"Tell her, Oren," Granddaddy said.

"I think that the power is there to bring it down, Brenda, but Mr. Sandman will fight to keep it. We can stand and fight along with him. If there's time."

"At least it's not Aunt Grace's fault," Latonya said.

" 'Tis, too," Brenda said. She pushed Latonya away and crawled into Granddaddy's lap. She hid her face in his shoulder.

"Brenda's right," Granddaddy said. "Grace's letters piled up with the others and primed His Honor to act. Stupid ideas are catching."

"Oren's right," Latonya said. "Let's go see what Mr. Sandman and the Goon Eye have to say."

"Godspeed in your mission," Granddaddy said. "You join them, Brenda. It might do you some good."

"Can I kill Aunt Grace?"

"No, you cannot kill Aunt Grace," Latonya said. "Put your shoes on, and we'll all go over and save Canfield Street."

They marched over like Onward Christian Soldiers. Blue made up a song:

> Fall in
> One two, one two
> Friends of Fred

151

Keep the faith.
Save the art
From friends of Grace.
Leave art alone.
Get outa our face!

While they were marching, they didn't believe anybody in the whole wide world would dare bust down the
art project. Brenda was perking up. She remembered
that the project was protected by her impatiens. They
were all infected by Latonya's positive attitude.

They found the Sandmans, the Goon Eye, and the children working to clean out the individual art pieces from
the houses. They were grim.

"The interview you saw was a tape," Susan Sandman
said. "Some city officials were out yesterday to take a
look, and I didn't like the expression on their faces."

"The order could come today, and bulldozers could
arrive without warning," the Goon Eye said. "We need to
take what work that's not nailed down to safer ground."

"My picture frames are all nailed down tight, and I'm
not going to let no bulldozer get them," Brenda yelled.

"I'll help you unnail your pictures, little Brenda."

"We appreciate you coming out in all this heat, people," Mr. Sandman said.

They worked right through the boiling afternoon. Mr.
Sandman's paintings and exhibits needed to be rescued
first. At some point Wesley showed up. She had seen the
interview. Her father had tried to call the mayor, but the
mayor wasn't taking calls. Latonya kept saying there

would be a reprieve and all the artwork would have to be returned to its natural place, but she moved stuff with the rest of them. Brenda's picture frames were hammered in to last for the lifetime of a vampire. They had to leave some behind that were her favorites. By dinnertime they were tired and thinking that the bulldozers would probably not come because it was too hot.

"I'm going to sleep the night here to make sure they don't," Brenda said.

"Mama and Jack won't let you stay unless me and Oren stay," Latonya said.

"You're all welcome to stay here," Susan Sandman said.

Latonya called home. Mama and Jack decided to come over and join them. Neighbors and friends from around the city and the 'burbs kept coming by to offer their support. By the time Mr. Shell and Ms. Pugh showed up, there was kind of a nervous party going on. Oren thought there just might be enough of them to take on bulldozers. There was strength and comfort in numbers. The adults took over the kitchen, and the young people had the living room. About two o'clock in the morning Oren crept off into a corner, curled up, and went to sleep.

When he woke, he thought there must be some kind of a storm coming, like the kind that blew Dorothy out of Kansas and into Oz. He couldn't think where he was. Daylight was coming through the window. He jumped up and ran through the empty house. Everyone was out-

side on the porch and front lawn with policemen holding them back. Oren watched hypnotized as a big monster ran over Brenda's impatiens. It was growling and
pushing toward a house that Mr. Sandman called the
Flavor of Detroit. The side of the house had been
painted different colors to represent streets and places,
past and present. If you looked, you could see old ceme-
teries underneath some of the buildings. Brenda had
helped Mr. Sandman put boats on the river. The house
was a map of the city, but it was more than the city.
There were no boundaries to Mr. Sandman's Detroit. Its
colors just kept wrapping around the surface of the
house. It took in and brought together streets and bright
things, places and people beyond the mile limits of the
city. Such a picture might be hard for some people to
see and understand, but it was all there. The monster
opened its huge mouth, and the Flavor of Detroit crum-
bled and disintegrated into exploding colors of dust.
The monster kept going, swallowing and riding over everything in its path.

Latonya was screaming, but the monster couldn't
hear. She was screaming that Brenda was inside the
house where the monster was headed. Oren started to
run. Jack and the Goon Eye were behind him. He ran up
the steps and into the living room. Brenda was desper-
ately trying to rip her picture frames from the wall. Oren
grabbed her around the waist. She punched him and
kicked him, but he managed to shift her securely into
Jack's open arms. The noise from the monster deadened
their shouts and screams. Jack held Brenda tightly. The

Goon Eye ripped one of her pictures from the wall. When they came outside, they saw that the crowd stood together holding hands in front of the porch. Aunt Grace, Dora, and police officers were in the line. The TV cameras were recording the scene. The monster was quiet, a piece of porch hanging from its mouth. Blue's brother came over to them, and his sad eyes told them the news.

"We have a court order, Brenda. We have to do it."

"Can't I rescue my pictures?" Brenda sobbed. She clutched the one the Goon Eye had rescued to her breast.

"We tried to get them off the wall last night. Skyler nailed them to be part of the house," Latonya said.

"Skyler is strong. He put them in and he can get them out. Please."

"I can get those pictures off the wall," Aunt Grace said.

Oren, Jack, the Goon Eye, and Aunt Grace went back in. Oren and Jack got one off the wall. Aunt Grace and the Goon Eye did the rest. Outside, with superhuman strength, Aunt Grace ripped the welcome picture off the porch.

When Brenda was safely in Mama's arms, the police broke up the line. The monster moved with opening jaws toward their house.

By evening there were men from the city sweeping up the remains. Blue, Whitey, Wesley, and all art lovers were gone. The Sandmans had gone inside their house to be alone with the Goon Eye and his children.

"I hate people who don't like our art," Brenda said.

"Well, you stop your spiteful hating, Miss," Latonya said.

"Can't you even let Brenda have a little honest hate?" Oren said.

"Why should I?" Latonya shot back. "Mr. Sandman is going on with his artwork, and so is Skyler. If artists can pick up and go again after a storm, then so can we, Oren Bell."

Mama and Jack put Brenda in the car and took her home. Oren and Latonya decided to walk.

"I wouldn't be surprised if Brenda is going into one of her states," Oren said.

"Where she stops talking or doing or eating?"

"She sneaks a little to eat, but she don't talk or do much," Oren said.

"She'll get over it. If she doesn't, Mama has the name of a psychologist that the Children's Hospital gave her after Brenda's last illness. We still have much to be thankful for, so let's go home and get back to some normal."

"What do we have to be thankful for?"

"We have our dear house and music studio on Fourth and Hancock Street, and you have your Fred Field."

It was true. He still had his Fred Field, but he had just seen how fast things you cared about could be swept away.

Chapter 16

○   ○   ○

"Oren Bell, where's your tie?"

"I'm playing ball."

"Not this morning. It's the twenty-seventh of August. Mama and Jack are taking off work so they can register us at a Catholic school."

"But we're not Catholic."

"It won't hurt you to be a little bit Catholic. Mama and Jack think it's the best school for us, and Ms. Pugh agrees. Now, put on your Sunday clothes."

"What about Brenda?"

"Brenda's staying with Granddaddy, but she will be registered. When school commences, she will be over her 'spoiled' disease and in the school seat assigned to her. I'll see to that."

"Good luck," Oren said.

Mama and Jack made a fine appearance. The head nun looked like she approved of them, and she was impressed with Latonya's school record. Mama assured her that Oren was being tutored. Mama described Brenda's abilities but left out her weirdness. It turned

157

out that you had to get dressed up and wear a tie every day of the week. Latonya believed the school was a place where she could shine. There wasn't going to be a single kid in the school that Oren knew. Latonya said he'd make new friends and that his old friends would be waiting for him every day at the Fred Field when he got home from school.

Mama and Jack took them to lunch to make up for ruining his day. It was a nice-enough eating place on the river. You could look out the window and see boats passing by while you were eating. Oren ordered a hamburger and fries like he always did when Jack took them out. Latonya gave him a dirty look and ordered a quiche, which was some kind of French food.

"Your mother and I want to talk to both of you about something important," Jack said. "Actually we have some good news and some bad news."

Oh, man. Jack had found some way to talk Mama into that stupid apartment. Oren would just pull a Brenda. He'd sit around all day and refuse to talk and do. Latonya was taking little bites out of her quiche like she expected Jack to bring up some happy surprise they'd enjoy hearing.

"Why don't you tell us the bad news first," Latonya said.

"We're going to move away from Fourth and Hancock Street." Mama came right to the point. "We need you two to help us with Brenda. We don't expect her to take the move well."

That was the understatement of the year. Oren decided to let Latonya give the first reply.

"Why are we moving away?" Latonya said calmly.

"The house has been condemned by the city," Jack said.

"It's been condemned for years," Oren said. "We pay rent to the city, and the city is glad to get it. The city expects us to throw away notices to move."

"I allow that next year we may have to move," Latonya said. "Or the year after that. Not this year. Not now."

"The building is going to be leveled in September of this year. In a few weeks," Jack said soberly. "The city intends to build low-income housing units on the property next spring."

"Units!" Oren said so loud that the people at the next table stared at them. "There isn't room for units on the space where our house stands."

"When our house is gone, there will be five empty lots to the corner," Mama said.

"That's the Fred Field!" Oren cried.

"The mayor is concerned about the children who have been killed in the city," Mama went on. "There's talk of naming the housing project the Fred Lightfoot Manor."

"Fred doesn't want no housing project named after him." Oren had such a lump in his throat that he could hardly get the words out.

"The first frost will end Brenda's impatiens anyway." There was a quaver to Latonya's voice when she said this. "Oren and I will do what we can to ease Brenda to this move."

Oren looked at his hamburger. He felt sick. Some poor cow had died to give him food, and he couldn't eat it. He was starting to sink like Brenda.

"What's the good news?" Latonya said.

"When Brenda told us we were Spiro Spill's only family, it appears that she was right. There are no descendants. No heirs. The court says that the treasure you children discovered in the two houses belongs to you."

Mama's voice was soft and low like she was giving them a little stroke to make them feel better. Oren didn't care about the treasure.

"How much are Spiro's gold records worth?" Latonya said.

"The market on gold changes," Jack said. "But the current appraisal comes out to about fifteen thousand dollars. Some of that money belongs to Blue and Whitey, because they helped find the records in the house next door. Your mother and I thought we'd start college funds for the three of you with the rest."

"That would please Spiro," Latonya said.

It didn't please Oren. A college fund wasn't going to balance out the loss of the Fred Field.

Mr. Shell was directing them toward a big final Labor Day concert in the Fred Field. While they were going at their music upstairs, Granddaddy had six students working on "The Bugle Rag" in the downstairs flat. Tuffcity was howling along with them, nearly on key. Brenda had gone off to a corner in the purple bedroom. Latonya intended to look in on her later. Latonya had a solo part in the concert, and it was hard to spend full time cozying a little sister who was existing on water and Chicken McNuggets. Oren had explained to Brenda that she wasn't the only one in the world who was getting dumped on.

Goon Eye came over after band practice and tried to get Brenda interested in art.

"Brenda, open up your ears and heart and listen to me. The musicians are going out howling, the ball players are going out playing, and us artists got to paint."

Brenda made no response. Granddaddy said if she regressed to Crayolas, it would be a hopeful sign. When Brenda got into one of her spells, it made Oren mad. Family and friends all had to rally around her weirdness and they couldn't wallow in their own misery.

"Brenda," the Goon Eye tried again. "Mr. Sandman is doing a mural on a whole wall in the Children's Museum. I'm helping, and so can you. Don't you worry. A bulldozer can't bring down a museum."

Oren believed that a bulldozer could bring down a museum, but it was best to give Brenda hope. The Goon Eye had to give up and leave, because Mrs. Sandman needed him to help with the children. If Spiro Spill returned, he would surely help Brenda. But instead Aunt Grace returned. At dinner she said, "Sarah, you know that I am not one to interfere, but it is time that you got some help for poor little Brenda. My Dede here is the same age and she is normal as apple pie."

Aunt Grace shoved Dede forward, and the child did look a little like an apple. Round face with a little black braid sticking straight up for a stem. Oren looked to see how the others were taking Aunt Grace's current invasion into their private affairs. Jack was ready to tell her off. Granddaddy was paying no attention. Mama and Latonya were considering, like some of Aunt Grace's meddlings might hold a grain of truth.

"Oren, go tell Brenda that dinner is ready," Mama said.

Oh, sure. He stood up. He'd have to carry the child to the table kicking and screaming. He always had to do what Mama said, or Jack would make him.

"Brenda, I've been watering your impatiens. You can repay me by carrying yourself into the dining room and pretending to eat some of the food. Dede is acting normal, and you are not. This is an embarrassment to our family pride. Please."

Brenda worked her way farther into the woodwork. When he returned to the dining room without her, the family didn't blame him.

"I'll take Brenda a dish of chicken nuggets later," Mama said.

Aunt Grace said, "Sarah, Chicken McNuggets won't solve the problem. You had better take Brenda to a doctor who specializes in weird children. If you do not heed my advice, Brenda could well be lost forever."

When Aunt Grace, Dink, and Dede finally left, the family held a meeting.

Granddaddy began. "Grace is the serpent in our family garden. I don't know why the Lord made serpents or people like Grace, but there must be some purpose for them in the balance of things."

"Does that mean that you think that Grace has a point?" Mama said.

"You miss my point, Sarah. By comparing our children to her children, she allows us to know how blessed we are. That is the best purpose I can find for listening to Grace. A genius child like Brenda doesn't march to the same tune as ordinary children. Give her time, love, and a few Chicken McNuggets and she'll come around."

"I agree with Bill," Jack said. "Brenda has lost a lot in her short lifetime, and she is about to lose more, but she has a loving family and she is basically a strong child."

"I don't agree with Grace on most things," Mama said. "But it wouldn't hurt to talk the problem over with a child psychologist."

"I don't want no doctor messing with Brenda's head," Granddaddy said.

"My vote stays with Bill," Jack said.

"What about you, Oren?" Latonya asked him. "I suppose you vote with the men."

The truth was, Mama held all the votes when it came to Brenda, but he thought for a minute. "I agree with what Jack and Granddaddy said, but Brenda does need something to help her through. Music and art don't seem to be enough, but I don't think she needs a head doctor. What Brenda needs is another ghost. I hope the Lord sees fit to send her one soon, because moving out of the best home we ever had is going to be hard on her soul."

"Spiro Spill was the one exception to the 'no such thing as ghosts' rule," Latonya said. "I don't believe in any but Spiro, but we could sure use the services of a good ghost."

"We'll continue with love and Chicken McNuggets for the time being," Mama said.

"Mama," Oren said, "if we move into an apartment, what happens to Skid and Tuffcity?"

"The apartment will accept an old cat that has been in the family for a while, but we will have to find a good home for Tuffcity."

They were going to lose their home, the Fred Field, and their dog. How was Latonya going to make something positive out of such a mess? It took her a minute.

"I believe that Blue Brown's family will give Tuffcity a loving home and that someday our pup will return to us. I believe that the new school will develop our potential. Our beautiful windows will cast their rosy light on our new home. Brenda will come around."

"And an ugly housing unit will spread over and wipe out the Fred Field," Oren said.

"You can't expect everything to always turn out perfect," Latonya said.

"Oren, feeling on edge all of the time improves your performance on the cornet," Granddaddy said. "I'm putting money aside to buy you a decent trumpet."

Oren was full of angry energy these days. There were

the final play-offs on the Fred Field and then the final concert.

When the Stooges played the Pistols, Oren knew the Stooges would win the last game for Fred, and that was a comfort. The Stooges had Latonya, who connected with the ball every time she came to bat.

The final concert was going to be what Mr. Shell termed a crowd pleaser. You did old tunes that the audience knew and you let them clap along. If notes got splatted, it was no big deal because the crowd was clapping, stomping, and maybe singing. It turned out that Mr. Fry knew how to play the accordion, so Mr. Shell worked it into the concert. Since his attack of indigestion Mr. Shell wanted to make everybody happy. The final ball game on the Fred Field was scheduled for the third of September. The final concert would be on the fifth. The big move would come two days later. Life as they knew it would be over, just as Oren Bell was becoming a manager, a leader, an athlete, and an excellent horn player.

Chapter 17

○   ○   ○

For the first time ever Latonya Bell struck out. The Stooges had lost. It shouldn't matter so much, but it did. Oren shook the Goon Eye's hand. "I wanted to win one for Fred, but your boys were the best," he said.

"I was trying to win one for Fred too," the Goon Eye said.

"Then I guess Fred won," Latonya said.

Dink hadn't been much of a help to the Stooges, but Oren was glad he'd let the kid play. Dede had done an acceptable job as a cheerleader. The two of them were moaning and groaning like their little hearts would break. Aunt Grace comforted them the best way she knew how.

"Dooley, you played a fine game. Dede, you cheered the team on when Brenda declined to even attend. With a little more support from Latonya, your team could have won."

"Latonya," Jack said, "if you ever change your mind about being a doctor, I'm sure the Tigers would sign you up, and I want to be your manager."

Mama and Jack sent out for an after-game dinner for

166

friends and family. They all sat in the dining room under the red windows to enjoy fried chicken. This time Mr. Sandman went into the purple room to talk to Brenda. She came out holding his hand. She played with her mashed potatos and tried to be polite. When dinner was over, Mr. Sandman turned to her.

"Brenda, I've been commissioned to do a sculpture of Fred to be placed in front of the new housing unit. Ms. Pugh has given me his school picture, but you're an artist and you knew Fred better than I. Could you help me?"

Brenda went to Mr. Sandman and gave him a hug. She didn't say a word. Oren knew that her hug was not a yes. She was telling him that she didn't know if she had the spirit for such a project.

"When you're ready, Brenda, we'll do it," Mr. Sandman said.

The last concert went by like one big long song. People from the neighborhood had brought guitars and washboards and mouth organs. Their homeless neighbors set up little tents. The singing went on into the night. When the Bell family and friends went inside, there were little bonfires of sing-alongs and rap sessions all over the Fred Field. Mama wished that there were room inside their house to take them all in, but Jack assured her it was a warm night and they all seemed to be having a good time. Oren, Latonya, Blue, Whitey, and the Goon Eye and his children finally bedded down in the upstairs flat. They could hear Mr. Fry downstairs playing what Wesley said was "The Lady of Spain" on his accordion. After that Ms. Pugh started playing her guitar, and Granddaddy accompanied her on the trumpet.

"What's that sad tune?" Oren whispered to Latonya.

"It's by a duo that was famous in the old days. I think it's called 'Bridge Over Troubled Waters.' "

"Do you think we'll hold up through moving day?"

"We have friends to help us."

"I'll take good care of Tuffcity," Blue said.

"I'll help him," Whitey promised.

"I'll be at the same school with you," Wesley said.

"How about you, Goon Eye?" Oren said. "You think you can find your way over to the new apartment to be with us?"

"I can find my way to anyplace in the world to keep with you guys, but having friends is not all it's about here."

"What is it about, Skyler?" Latonya said.

"It's about little Brenda and how she takes the move. Mr. Sandman's been an artist for a long time and he's used to people dumping on his art. Brenda doesn't understand how when your work gets swallowed and crunched by monsters, you have to get up and start creating something new. We couldn't even move her out of her room to be with us tonight."

"The Goon Eye is right," Oren said. "A new apartment with no purple room could sink her so low, she could never rise up again. We got to be more than friends for her."

"We have to be a bridge over for Brenda," Latonya said.

Chapter 18

○   ○   ○

There were many friends to help them move. Tuffcity was excited. He didn't know that when the excitement was over, he would be going home with Blue. Skid was sleeping snug on Granddaddy's lap like it was any other day. Brenda stayed in the purple bedroom. Jack said they would move the bedroom furniture last. Aunt Grace pulled up in front. They didn't need her mouth, but they could use her truck.

"The thing that amazes me," Oren confided to Latonya, "is how Mr. Sandman can work alongside Aunt Grace even though she said bad things about his work. Mr. Sandman doesn't swear at her. He's polite."

" 'He that is slow to anger is better than the mighty, and he who rules his spirit can take a city.' "

"Did you make that up?"

"It was a message from the Bible last week in Sunday school. People like Mr. Sandman, Abraham Lincoln, and me choose to take our attitudes from the Bible."

Jack and Aunt Grace took the trucks back and forth with furniture, and Mama and Ms. Pugh went along to show them where everything went. The Goon Eye went

with the trucks because he was so strong. The rest of
the movers elected to stay with the house until the bit-
ter end. Granddaddy and Skid would be moved out in
the chair. The Sandmans went up in the attic looking for
art objects. Latonya was busy scrubbing under all the
places where the furniture had been, but even on her
knees she gave orders.

"Why does a house that is going to be bulldozed
down have to be so clean, Latonya?" Whitey com-
plained.

"Would you go to meet your Maker with a dirty face?"

"The Lord is not as particular as you, Latonya,"
Granddaddy said. "You missed a spot inside the fireplace, girl."

Oren was having the most miserable day of his life.
How could he leave the Fred Field behind? Did anybody
care? All they talked about was how to move the bloody
red windows. They should have called themselves
Friends of the Windows.

Mr. Shell was closing down the music studio. When
the end was near, Oren went upstairs to give the three-
minute warning to the Music Man. Wesley was helping
him. The two of them were drumming out musical ar-
rangements with Wesley's drumsticks on the thick wood
around the windows.

"Latonya says it's nearly time to go."

"The acoustics are very good in this room," Mr. Shell
said.

"I could jam here forever," Wesley said.

"The man who built this house used this upstairs flat

171

for a music studio," Mr. Shell said. "Nearly a hundred years of music within these walls. If we stayed, I would rip out Grace's white carpeting. C'mon, Oren, beat out *The 1812 Overture* with Wesley and me on the woodwork before we go."

Finally it was the end. Blue took Tuffcity into the Brown family car. They rode off, and the pup never looked back.

Granddaddy's chair was in Jack's final truckload. They had moved the bedroom furniture from out and around Brenda. Jack was driving the truck, and Mama was driving the van.

"Oren, I elect to go with you and the women in the van," Granddaddy said. "You pick up the cat and settle him on my lap. My legs have gone to sleep. I'm going to tell Latonya to put Skid on a diet."

"Oren," Latonya said, "after you settle them, you fetch Brenda."

"Latonya and I will help you," Mama said. "We need to give a final check through the rooms to see if we missed anything."

Didn't they think he needed a little time alone on the Fred Field? He had stayed out on the field until Mama called him in, the night before. Blue's brother had given the field a final patrol in his police car, and Oren had exchanged salutes with the officer. Maybe it was better that he left it at that.

The living room looked big with no furniture, and the late-afternoon sun gave the bare wood floors a bright finish. Latonya must have given them a really big final polish.

"Listen to me, Oren," Latonya said in a tired voice. "We didn't have a place before this house took us in. Those rooms that we slept and ate in when we were little kids were just for passing through. When we came to rest here, we had a place."

"I know that."

They went together into the purple bedroom.

"C'mon, Brenda, it's time to go," Oren said.

"You'll just make Mama and Jack feel bad if you persist," Latonya said.

She got up from her corner and followed him out of the purple bedroom. The three Bells solemnly marched out of the house.

"Brenda, don't you want to say good-bye to your impatiens? They're blooming nicely," Oren said. "I said good-bye to my field last night and felt some better for it."

"No."

"Why?"

"Because impatiens have shallow roots, and you can never depend on things with shallow roots. They don't stand up to invaders the way they should. Jack should have never given me those seeds. It's all Jack's fault. All these terrible disasters are Jack's fault."

They were all encouraged by this. Brenda hadn't said so many words for a long time. Jack took the blame like a man. He walked over to the Fred Field and pulled up

Brenda's sign. If they left it, the city would throw it away. The sign contained good rules to live by.

There would be kids playing on the field tomorrow and the next day, until the housing project took up its space. The players would remember the rules for a while. Maybe Oren could take a bus over and bat some balls and shoot some hoops. He got into the van with Mama, Latonya, Brenda, Granddaddy, and Skid. Jack moved his truck out and waved for them to follow. The Bell-Daniels family left their home on Fourth and Hancock Street.

"It doesn't look like a new place," Oren said.

"These are old historic buildings, remember, Oren?" Latonya said. "See the gaslights in front of each unit? Only the insides are new. Our building was the laboratory for the biggest drug company in America. Medicines and vitamins to cure and tone up a nation were thought up within these walls. Take pride in your new place, Oren Bell."

Jack must have known what was going on inside Brenda's head. "I know we have a small patch of lawn, Brenda, but we will plant something here that has strong roots."

After the rest had gone inside, Latonya told Oren that they were not allowed to plant stuff with strong roots. Jack shouldn't have given Brenda false hope.

Once Aunt Grace and her children went home, inside, the mood lightened up.

"Man, this is some beautiful place you got here," Blue said.

"The dining room table fits," Latonya allowed.

"Hey," the Goon Eye shouted up the stairs to his children, "no jumping on the new beds."

The first big action was hanging the red windows. Oren took Brenda upstairs to her new room, because she didn't want to watch. The room had white walls. Oren had always thought white was kind of a nothing color.

"A lot of space for you to hang pictures, Brenda."

Brenda wasn't listening. There were new twin beds with fancy bedspreads that looked like they shouldn't be mussed. The carpeting was soft. Brenda found a corner and took possession of it. She seemed to be content to sulk there, so Oren went across the hall to check out his room.

Not bad. He could see the Belle Isle Bridge from his window, and he could see a passing freighter. He could see across the river to Windsor, Ontario, Canada. He would be watching this neat stuff every day of his life. He decided to lie down on his new bed and just look out his new window and observe life going by. It made him feel a little guilty to feel satisfied.

"Oren, you get down here," Latonya called. "We need you."

When the windows were secure over the fireplace, they stood back and admired them.

They were all tired, so the moving party broke up early. The Goon Eye, his children, and the Sandmans were the first to leave. Blue wanted his folks to go home, because he had a dog waiting there for him.

The family was alone in the new place. Mama and Jack went upstairs to say good night to Brenda. Latonya pulled Granddaddy's Hide-A-Bed out, and she and Oren made it up for him. After that she fixed milk and cookies for Brenda and followed Oren up to the third level. They both knew that Brenda wouldn't touch the food, but Latonya had to try.

Oren was surprised and happy to see that Skid was sleeping on his bed. Granddaddy wouldn't mind if Skid left him for Oren. He put out the light, whipped off his clothes, leaped into bed, and snuggled down beside his purring old cat. In the dark he could still see the lights on the river. This was the first room to himself that he had ever had. First night that he hadn't slept on a lumpy sofa. He would take a bus to the Fred Field in the morning.

"Oren Bell, come by us immediately," Latonya called.

What now? He went across the hall and looked in. Brenda was sitting up in bed and wolfing down the milk and cookies. She had a big smile on her face. That was weird, but not worth getting out of bed to see.

"What's the matter?"

"Brenda's 'sad' sickness is over, and she won't tell me why."

"Tell Latonya why, Brenda."

"I won't tell."

"She'll tell us tomorrow, or maybe never," Oren said. "I'm going back to bed."

"Oren, Latonya, I want one of you to call Mr. Sandman and tell him that I will help him make a beautiful sculpture of Fred. A statue that will last forever. We will forge it out of stuff that has roots. We need to get started on it. Our Fred statue will sit in front of the Fred Housing Project on the Fred Field, or the Children's Museum in Detroit, or maybe we will put it in the Worldwide Hall of Fame."

"This shifting from low straight up to high has me worried. If there was some reason for it, I could rest easy," Latonya said.

"Mr. Sandman has gone to bed. You can tell him tomorrow, Brenda," Oren said. "Go to sleep, Latonya. I'll find out the reason tomorrow."

He returned to his own room and climbed into his bed. He was tired and he hadn't prayed for a long time, but he thought a few words to the Lord might be in order. Praying had been easier last year when he had been innocent. Now he wasn't sure what was good and what was bad in his life. The lines were getting all fuzzy.

Dear Lord,
Thank you for the summer of this year of
our lives.
Latonya and Mama had their wedding
and Jack got to be a Bell-Daniels.
I made new friends, known to you as Skyler Sims
and the Sandmans.
You helped me bring Fred's murderer to justice

with the help of Skid and Tuffcity, who are
your creatures,
and the red windows, who might be from
the devil.
We all enjoyed some glory on the Fred Field.
No offense, Lord,
but you did throw us a few curves.
You gave us the Fred Field and then you took
it away,
which I guess is your privilege.
Brenda lost her art project and purple room,
and her impatiens didn't do much to cut the loss.
Aunt Grace says that Brenda is a hypermaniac
depressed child,
but you and me know, Lord,
that Brenda's real problem is
understanding why
ships have to sink and buildings have to fall
and why nothing good or bad stays the same
forever.
I'm holding back my judgment on the River
Apartment and the new school.
I know you'll do the best you can, Lord.
Your friend, Amen.
Oren Bell
P.S.
It's great that Skid is sleeping with me, but
I'd like to get my dog back as soon as you can
manage it.

He fell asleep immediately like he had been sucked into a dark hole in the sky. When words and pokes woke him up, he was swimming through the dark hole to get to the little fireflies of light on the other side.

"Oren, wake up."

"What, Brenda? I was having an interesting sleep."

"Don't you want to hear about my new ghost?"

"What?" He sat straight up in bed.

"I found it in my new white room. It was so white, I could hardly see it at first."

"Is it a boy or a girl ghost?"

"I don't know that yet."

"What's its name?"

"I don't know that yet, but it belongs to this building and stays in my room. I told it that I will be busy sculpting and painting and easing into my new school, but I promised to befriend it and do what I could to help it and keep it company."

"Did you tell Latonya?"

"No. My new ghost isn't strong enough to meet Latonya yet."

"Well, you tell her as soon as you see fit. She'll rest easier. Now, get back to bed. You're disturbing the cat."

It was pleasant lying on his bed by the window and watching the harbor lights. It was sort of like he was on a ship himself. He thought of a good notion to go to sleep by:

Once upon a time there was a special place where peo-

ple could get together, play ball, and make music. That place was called the Fred Field.

As he fell asleep, he could feel the red windows watching over every one of them, even Brenda's ghost.

BARBARA HOOD BURGESS is the author of *Oren Bell*. She lives in Livonia, Michigan, and has four grown children and six grandchildren. She recently received her B.A. degree from Wayne State University. She has written musical theater projects and operettas for church, scout, and children's groups, and now enjoys making school visits to talk about writing.

She knows the neighborhood where *The Fred Field* takes place very well because one of her sons, Chris, used to live in a haunted house like the Bell family's at the corner of Fourth and Hancock streets.